"Pierly" Outer Banks
By
Jennifer Shenberger
&
Greg Smrdel

Book One of the Nags Head Beach Series

Milepost 11 Publishing - 2019

Other books by Greg Smrdel:

Hurricane Izzy - An OBX Story

Home Sweet Outer Banks Home?

Home Sweet Outer Banks Home: The Story Continues

Blackbeard's Outer Banks Treasure

The Andy Griffith Show Complete Trivia Guide, 2nd edition

A Novel Idea: Fiction Writing Made Easy

Trivia Night: Answers You Wished You Knew, Volumes 1-3

Ray Turner's Morning MindBender

Coming soon:

Murder in Kill Devil Hills

One Day I'll Forget the Corolla Horses (working title)

Find all the books at
www.amazon.com/author/gregsmrdel

Other Projects by Jennifer Shenberger:

La Cucaracha Motel Comics

Coming Soon:

Suburban Flamingo Comics
Marin Michaels Mystery Series

Greg's Dedication

"Pierly" Outer Banks is dedicated to all those that have read my previous books. It is because of ya'll that I continue to write. This book is also dedicated to Ami Cannon Hill and Jonathan Dietz of Muse Originals OBX in Kitty Hawk, Jamie at Downtown Books in Manteo, GeeGee at Buxton Village Books in Buxton, Cory at Bluegrass Island Trading Co in Manteo, Island Bookstores on the Outer Banks and the Cotton Gin. These people have made it possible for everyone to read my work locally by stocking my books on their shelves. I owe ya'll a debt of gratitude.

Jennifer's Dedication

This book is dedicated to all the sucky jobs I have had before and during the writing of this book. It is because of you that I write. I would name companies but I am afraid of legal trouble so YOU KNOW WHO YOU ARE, will have to suffice. On a more serious note, this book is dedicated to my husband for letting me do this, my parents for not laughing when I told them I was doing this, and JB, LS, AS for just going with it

Greg's Author's Note:

This is a different kind of book than I have ever written before. My very good friend Jennifer Shenberger and I collaborated on this one. I wrote one chapter, and based on what I had written, she would write the next. And visa versa. It was a lot of fun, and very challenging, all at the same time. Many emails went back and forth during this project. It was crazy! It is my hope that we do one of these again in the future! (SPOILER ALERT!! As it turns out - WE WILL!)

As always, I want to thank my lovely wife Char for her unwavering belief in me. I couldn't do what I do without her. I also want to thank each and every one of you that have bought my books, and continue to do so. It is my passion and I will continue to write as long as I have an audience that enjoys what I create.

Till next time!

Greg Smrdel
Manteo, NC 2019

Jennifer's Author's Note:

This is a different kind of book than I have ever written before, mainly because I have never written a book before. My (I don't know if very good friend is appropriate) friend and comedy father Greg Smrdel and I wrote this book together. He likes to use bigger words like collaborated but I don't know many big words so I will just have to settle for using several smaller ones. I hope you are good with that. For the most part I wrote the whole book while Greg (also known as Papa Smurf, Herkey Smrdel, sometimes Francisco) sat in his underwear and drank beer. He says he has written other books but honestly, I don't know that I believe him. This is mainly a test to see if he will actually read what I write. (*Greg's note: Um, no, I didn't read this, but someone told me about it*)

This project was a ton of fun. It was completely improvised and was fun to put each other's characters in situations and see what the other person would do with it. Sometimes it went how I thought and other times I was completely thrown. See, I just used completely and fun twice — I don't know a lot of words. If you bought this book I thank you from the bottom of my heart. Now I can buy a Thesaurus.

Thank you.

Jennifer Shenberger
Johnstown, OH 2019

Chapter One. Bob

Baa. That's the sound I hear in my head each morning as I drive to work. Baa. Baa. On Mondays it's usually twice as loud; but on this particular Monday, it seemed louder still. BAA! BAA! BAA! Look at all us sheep mindlessly driving to work, I thought. Every day, it's the same people in the same cars, all heading in the same direction. All zombies preparing to give some faceless corporation, or some abusive boss, another 8-10 hours of our lives. But who was I to judge? I wondered, I'm doing the exact same thing. BAA! BAA! BAA! BAA!

I came up on a stop light as it went from green to yellow. Apparently the guy behind me in the shiny, new Land Rover was the type A sort, laying on the horn, expecting me to speed up before the light went from yellow to red. But instead, I slowed to a stop. I had long ago come to the realization that my commute into work is often times longer than the commute back home. In the morning I'm in no hurry to get to my destination, but going back home? Well, that was a different story….

I sat at the light, the guy in the Land Rover behind me, just inches from my back bumper, as I thought back to the past weekend. The weekend was great, as it often is. After work Friday, I had met up with some friends at the Comedy Club downtown. We all went to see my favorite comedian; Jake Johannsen. It was a great night, the perfect way to wrap up a stressful week! Saturday, I picked up my former in-laws to take them out to dinner to celebrate Father's Day a day early. My wife Linda, sadly, died 3 years ago from breast cancer, but I have still stayed in touch with Sandy and Babe; her parents. They were as much a part of my life as they ever were, even after Linda had passed. In fact, they're the ones that keep reminding me that even though Linda is gone, life goes on and I should start dating again. Maybe they're right. Maybe I should, I thought. But, I don't know. It had never felt right.

Now, Sunday was reserved for stand up paddle boarding, one of my favorite new hobbies. I had watched some people doing it on the Outer Banks of North Carolina, so I thought I would give it a try. I took to it like an alcoholic to drink. One time out and I was hooked.

Just as a smile started to come across my face as I thought the wonderful thoughts of the weekend, I was startled out of my daydream by a loud car horn. The jerk in the Land Rover was leaning on his horn the instant the light went back to green. With that I put the Jeep through its paces. First gear, second gear, third gear and finally to fourth gear, never making it all the way to sixth, as I continued my commute to work at 35 MPH, not a single 1 MPH faster than the posted speed limit. That will further steam the Type A jerk, I thought, as a smile returned to my face.

Twenty minutes later, I pulled into the parking lot at work. My stomach dropped to my feet, as it did 5 days a week, knowing that this non-descript building would be my prison until 5 pm today, a very long 10 hours from now. I was once asked where the building was located in which I worked. I simply answered "I don't really know, I leave home and just drive until the dread rises to its highest level, then I turn left into a parking lot and there I am!"

I got out of my car and made my way to the back door. I always went in through the back. Too many "way too happy" people gather in the front. I always thought these people not too intelligent to be this happy while giving away a large chunk of their life to this place each and every day. Week after week. Month after month. Year after…..well, you get the picture.

Using my key fob to gain entrance through the back door, I tried to make my way down a side hallway before being seen by my boss, but I wasn't so lucky on this Monday morning.

"Hey Bob!" My boss yelled out. "How's the sausage business?" Same damn joke every….single….damn….day. My boss thinking he's so damn clever just because my last name is Evans.

"Yeah, good one boss" I replied back, not even trying to hide my disdain as I muttered "jerk" under my breath. Like I never heard that joke in my life before…..

I grabbed a cup of coffee in the kitchen, keeping my gaze directed down at my feet, trying hard not to engage in conversation with anyone, when I was approached by one of the "too happy to be here people. "Hey Bob, why do you always use a disposable coffee cup rather than bring one from home like everyone else?"

"Oh, that's a simple question to answer," I said. "It's so I have one less thing to carry out of here when I finally walk out for the last time." Thankfully he didn't know how to respond.

I then made my way over to my desk in my windowless cubicle, lit only by the overhead fluorescent lights. No view of the outside world on a day that was shaping up to be gorgeous. Or at least as beautiful a day as Cleveland, Ohio can provide. A depressing way to spend your day couldn't be anymore possible, I thought.

Time to sell some crap to the world that doesn't really need it, I said to myself as I flipped the power button to the on position on my computer, and up came my happy place….

Chapter Two. Charlie

Every morning I have the same routine: alarm goes off, check the surf forecast, watch the sunrise from my paddle board, then go to work at the pier restaurant. Oh, and I own the restaurant. No one ever believes I own it. Mostly because the restaurant is named Chuck's Grub & Tiki Bar.

My name is Charlie, named after my father Charles, who was apparently hoping for a boy, but that is another story. Anyway, I decided to embrace years and years of "What's up, Chuck? Get it? Upchuck, like barf?" As if I'm also dumb. So now, the restaurant.

I cherish my mornings in the restaurant. There is something about being the first one in the building that seems magical. I have to say, it's one of my favorite times of day. The light leaks in through the windows, letting a little bit of the outside in. I can still feel the ocean water cool on my skin. A cup of coffee and the smell of salt air is all I need in that moment. I also have a mug that says the same thing. I'm a sucker for coffee mugs.

"Hey, Chuck!"

And the moment is over. "Danny. What can I do for you?"

"One of those dang webcams is blocked. Want me to go ahead and fix 'er?"

Danny is a great maintenance guy but he is lacking in the communication department. "We have webcams?"

"Uh, yeah, boss-lady. I put in like 4 of them, reckon it be 'bout a month ago now," said Danny. "It streams live on some website. Least ways, that's what they told me."

"Excuse me, what?" I could not help but picture some sort of creepy website where people do gross things without clothes with other people who may or may not have clothes on. All the while, knowing that people are watching. And who knows about their clothing decisions. I know one thing, they probably have cats. Lots of cats.

I had to check it out. At least it was an Outer Banks website. And a lot of other business owners were involved too. I just needed to know where the cameras were. I love people and I love my restaurant, but I also like my privacy.

I yelled back to Danny, "So these things only go on during business hours, right?"

"No ma'am. Those cameras, they be on all day, everyday," he said.

"Perfect." I could not have been more sarcastic. The webcams are set up in all my favorite places: the pier, the deck, and the surrounding beach. I guess that's great if you love cats and the beach. "I have to be honest, Danny, I feel a little violated."

Danny giggled a little bit. "Violated, that's just crazy. Just 'cause I saw you pick your wedgie out your butt on camera yesterday, that don't mean everyone seen you pick your wedgie on camera."

I laughed because I thought I should, but it still felt a little weird. I needed to move on. I am not going to let this get in the way of my day. After all, today is Monday. The day I play the ukulele at the Tiki Bar.

Maybe Danny is right. Maybe no one is watching.

Chapter Three. Bob

I have three computer monitors on my desk. One for spreadsheets and the like. One for sales orders, and one for my happy place: The webcam at the Nags Head Fishing pier. Honestly, that's where most of my attention is focused throughout most days.

Being an orthopedic shoe broker, selling orthopedic shoes wholesale to orthopedic shoes stores is not exactly what I had in mind when I was little and people asked me what I wanted to be when I grew up. But in the words of the Boss, Springsteen, not the jackass making sausage jokes everyday thinking he's hilarious, "Somewhere along the line I slipped off track."

I knew my line of work was ridiculous when we announced to the world our new product line of orthopedic flip-flops. Our slogan? "You can still be beboppin' while you're flip-floppin'!" That one just edged out "You can still go on beach marches with your fallen arches!" Told you it was ridiculous....

There she is, the girl that works at the Nags Head pier. She appears to be a server at the restaurant, but the way she lingers at all the tables tells me she's something more. I love watching the waves of the Atlantic and the surfers and kayakers and the sun tanners. But most of all, if I'm honest with myself, this girl at the pier is the reason I watch the webcams. I call her America. Not after our country, but rather after the folk rock band formed in England in the 70's. You know, they had a huge hit with "A Horse With No Name." To me, she was the girl with no name. I thought it particularly cute, when America, not knowing someone 650 miles away was watching, picked her wedgie.

Now, I don't want to come across as a total miserable lout. I am thankful for at least one thing on this Monday. I get to leave early today. My cat, Boris, has been marking his territory around the yard lately, spraying all the Rhododendrons. Letting the feral cats in the neighborhood know, "I am king of this woody plant jungle!" So I need to take Boris to the vet to be fixed.

I know. Single guy with a cat. But Boris is good company and he is, as far as I'm aware, the only paddle-boarding cat in North East Ohio. He loves standing at the nose of my paddleboard while we circle Geauga Lake on Sundays in the summer.

A couple of strange things occurred today before I was able to pack up and leave. Firstly, the boss, this time the jerk who makes stupid sausage jokes everyday, not Springsteen, swung by my desk to remind me to take my laptop home with me since I'm leaving early. I mean, really? When's the last time you've ever heard of an orthopedic shoe emergency? EXACTLY!!!! Jerk....

Secondly, as I was just about to turn off my three monitors to leave for the vet, I noticed that America was in some sort of heated exchange with someone. This seemed to be out of character to me. I've never witnessed her ever being in an argument with anyone before. And trust me, I've logged a lot of hours on this webcam to know.

That's the trouble with the webcams, I can only surmise what is happening while watching through the "virtual window." I don't really know what is going on. Hell, I don't even know America's real name.

Oh well, time to take Boris to the vet and get the hell out of here. You can be sure that my ride home will take half the time it took me to get here.....

Chapter Four. Charlie

GET OVER YOURSELF. Those were the words I painted on my coffee mug and they were aimed directly at the turd wagon in my restaurant. Why sweep it under the rug, when you can say it on a mug? It's the truth and it's also the name of my side business.

The idea is not wholly original. I stole it from my mom. In my eyes, she revolutionized the cross-stitching business. She once told me my dog died on a quote pillow. It took her two weeks to make it but I should've figured out the dog died sooner.

Anyway, mugs are quicker and more useful.

So, this turd wagon walks in and says, "I want to talk to Chuck."

Clearly this jackoff has no idea who he is talking to. "I'm Chuck, but you can call me Charlie." We shook hands and I immediately felt the need to scrub them down. A lot.

"I'm from Dare County…"

Oh great, this is all I need. We already have webcams, what else does this guy want?

"We have interest from a few investors for the pier."

"Stop right there. I'm not interested in selling. Ever."

"You may not have a choice unless you want to buy the pier, too."

"I own this property," I said.

"You lease the building, you don't own the pier."

I had heard enough. I grabbed my mug. He stopped talking. He stared at the mug and then at me. His eyes shifted back-and-forth several times.

"Are you telling me to get over myself?"

"If the orthopedic flip-flop fits." I mean, seriously, who wears orthopedic flip-flops?

"You have some nerve, Chuck or Charlie or whatever your name is."

I grabbed a muffin from the counter and slapped some icing on top. "Here, you seem like the kind of guy who would put icing on a muffin and call it a cupcake."

"What is that supposed to mean?"

"You can see yourself out."

About that time Danny walked through the door. "What the gold-darned just happened?" He asked.

"Nothing." I tried not to look upset, but at that moment, I wasn't sure of anything. The only thing I did know was that turd wagon's cologne was stuck in my nose hairs.

"Don't look like nothin' to me," said Danny.

This is going to take a lot of mugs to explain. My hands hurt just thinking about it.

"I'm taking my paddleboard out for a little bit. I need to clear my head."

"You can't go out there now. It be way too rough," said Danny.

"Danny, I just need to be alone right now. Let me be."

"Reckon you best be careful," he said.

I took my paddleboard and headed for the ocean. It's the one place I felt safe. It's the one place I could clear my head. I knew I would figure something out, I just needed to let the ocean speak to me. The water ran over my toes as I debated the sanity of taking my board out in these conditions. Without much debate, I lunged into the water. The rest was a blur.

Chapter Five. Bob

"Gawd I hate this! Why can't any kind of doctor, whether people or animal, EVER be on time?" I thought to myself.

I got off work early for this cat appointment, hoping it will go quickly so I can enjoy a little bit of me time at home earlier than I would on a normal work day. But apparently that's not gonna happen. Story of my life.

Finally, the vet tech calls Boris back for the procedure and tells me that it will take less than 30 minutes. Boris, however, won't be ready to go home for at least a couple of hours. Since they're open till 9 tonight, it wouldn't be a problem to come back later to pick him up.

I decide since I have time to kill, I'd run up to the Heinens grocery store, grab a steak as big as my head, along with corn-on-the-cob and a big potato, which I will throw in the microwave. Oh, and a six-pack of Pacifico. Can't forget my favorite beer to wash it all down!

At home, the steak and corn are on the grill. The potato in the microwave, the ice cold Pacifico at my side, I decide to open my laptop. Not to check for any "orthopedic shoe emergencies," you understand. That just is not gonna happen. "Dumb, ass boss" I said aloud to no one. "He is just dumb enough to think I actually care." But rather, I open it to see what is happening with America. When I shut down the computer at work she was in a heated exchange with some dude. Being a little over an hour later, I wondered if that was still going on.

The pier is clear. America is nowhere in sight. Not many on the pier at all actually. Those that are, seem to be bundled up. Not a normal scene in late July on the Outer Banks. The wind seems to be blowing pretty heavily out of the Northeast. In fact as the webcam pans another 45 degrees southward I see the Red "No Swimming" Flag posted. Judging by the angriness of Mother Ocean, you would have to be a complete moron to be out in the water. Just last week alone, the Outer Banks lifesaving crew pulled four people out of the Atlantic. Certainly, one would think, others would take heed of that news and act accordingly.

The webcam pans yet another 45 degrees southward. Wait! What's that? There IS someone in the water. Are you effing kidding me? I thought. Who the hell would be that ridiculously stupid? As the pier webcam pulls in for a close up of the distant object, I realize that moron was America! What the hell is she doing out there?!?! I always assumed she was smarter than that....

What I saw next chilled me to the bone. Amid the chop of the gray, angry Atlantic waters, a very obvious dorsal fin appeared right next to America's paddleboard. That did not just happen.....

Chapter Six. Bob

I think I'm gonna be sick.....

Chapter Seven. Charlie

Please tell me that is a dolphin fin, please tell me that is a dolphin fin. I was trying my hardest to convince myself (and the shark) that it was a dolphin. I didn't buy it and neither did the shark. What are the odds that two turd wagons show up to ruin my life in one day? He kept circling. I had nowhere to go. Trying to find protection, I climbed on my paddleboard. Maybe he would bite the board and not me.

The waves were getting more intense. It was getting harder to stay on the board. If only I had listened to Danny. Only an idiot would be out here in this weather. What the hell was I thinking?

The shark fin disappeared. I looked everywhere. Nothing. I felt a sense of relief but was still afraid to move. The fin disappearing meant he wasn't circling anymore, but it also meant I had no idea where he was. Okay, I will stay on my board until he is gone. Then I'll swim to shore and never do something this stupid again.

I contemplated trying to paddle in but was afraid to put my hands in the water. I didn't have a choice. The waves tossed me in the water. Another wave pushed me down even further. I fought to reach the surface. Still attached to my board, we found each other along with the surface. Things seemed to settle for a moment. I climbed back on the board when suddenly an incredible force came from the water – it flipped me off the board. I was in a fight with a shark. I started wailing and punching. Forget eyes and gills, I was aiming for anything. My board was pulled under the water. My leash pulled me down with it. I kicked trying to free myself from the board and the shark. The leash snapped. I finally surfaced. The shark was gone. At least I couldn't see him.

I knew I needed to get to shore. I started swimming with what strength I had left. I looked behind to see a huge wall of water chasing me down. Mother Ocean was showing no sympathy or remorse for what had just happened. I swam harder. I looked back again to see her regurgitate my paddleboard and it was headed straight for me. I tried to swim out of its path. The current pulled me in and...

Chapter Eight. Bob

"911. What is your emergency?"

"Hi, my name is Bob Evans…."

"Like the sausage guy?"

"Yes, like the sausage guy, but…"

"Are YOU the sausage guy?"

"No, I'm not the sausage guy! He's dead. Or if he isn't dead he'd be like a hundred years old by now. Do I sound like I'm a hundred? Or dead?"

"Sorry sir, what is your emergency?"

"There's a girl being attacked by a shark!"

"Sir, have you been drinking? There are no sharks in Lake Erie."

"Not Lake Erie you idiot! In the Atlantic Ocean!"

"Sir. This is Cleveland 911. We are not located on the Atlantic Ocean."

"No…..no….no. It's America. She's being attacked by a shark in Nags Head, North Carolina!"

"Sir, are you sure you haven't been drinking? Now you're telling me our country is being attacked by a shark?"

"No! America is a girl!"

"Now we're getting somewhere. America is a girl in Nags Head getting attacked by a shark."

"Yes! We're wasting time here!"

"Yes sir. What's America's last name?"

"I don't know her personally. America's probably not even her real first name. It's just what I call her."

"You call a girl you don't even know America and she's being attacked by a shark in Nags Head, North Carolina?"

"Yes! Yes! It's a long story and I don't really have time to explain it now. Can you just connect me to the lifesaving service or to the 911 for Nags Head please?"

"Well sir, it's not as simple as that. Do you know their emergency number?"

"Yes! Same as yours. It's 911!"

"Sorry sir. It's not as simple as that. I will have to Google their emergency number."

"Please hurry!"

"Here we are. I will connect you over now."

"Finally! Thank you!"

"911. What is your emergency."

"Hi, yes, thank you. My name is Bob Evans…"

"Like the sausage guy?"

"Yes, like the sausage guy…"

"Are YOU the sausage guy?"

"Oh my God! Just listen! On the south side of the Nags Head Pier, America is getting attacked by a shark!"

"Sir, have you been drinking? You're saying our country is being attacked by a shark?"

"No, a girl named America! I mean I don't know what her real name is, can you just please send someone to the pier?"

"How do you know this girl is being attacked by a shark sir?"

"I'm watching it on the webcam. It's happening as we speak!"

"Ok, we will dispatch the Coast Guard, Lifesaving Service and the Nags Head Police. Tell me where exactly this is all occurring and what exactly is happening."

……with that the webcam went out….

Chapter Nine. ABC 11

The scene, Nags Head pier was not so calm a few hours ago. With red "no swimming" flags waving, a local woman decided to brave the surf. She soon got much more than she bargained for. We go live to the pier with Duffy Dixon. Duffy?

"Thanks, Frank. Nags Head pier is usually the site of happy families playing on the beach, surfers trying to catch a few waves, and fishermen trying to reel in the next big catch. The scene earlier today was much different when local restaurant owner, Charlie Foster, nearly drowned in the ocean. I have with me not only an eyewitness, but also the man that helped save her life, local filmmaker, Ollie Frakingham. Ollie, describe what happened out there today."

"Thanks, Duffy. It's FARKingham. Ollie Farkingham." Getting no reaction from Duffy, he continued.

"Well, we were filming a scene with a mechanical shark when I saw Charlie struggling in the water. There was no way she was going to get back to shore on her own so we sent the mechanical shark over to help her out."

"It's my understanding that you lost control of the shark. Is that true?"

"Yes. The water was so rough that we totally lost control of the shark for a few moments. We were able to regain the radio signal and get Charlie safely to shore just in time for the coast guard to show up and take over."

"Were you afraid that she would think she was being attacked by the shark?"

"I was just trying to get her out of the water. But we did get the whole ordeal on tape. You better believe I want that in my next movie."

"You heard it here folks, an almost tragic day at the pier turns into movie gold when a mechanical shark saves the life of local restaurant owner, Charlie Foster.

Duffy Dixon reporting live for ABC 11 at Nags Head pier. Back to you Frank.

Chapter Ten. Charlie

I wasn't in the mood for much of anything. In a matter of hours, the video had gone viral. Ollie Frakingham wasted no time posting it to every social media site he could think of. Every news outlet had picked it up. I was getting interview requests from anyone and everyone. I didn't ask for this.

"Dude, you are famous. I swear your mug is everywhere," said Danny.

As much as I usually want to slap Danny when he talks, something he said stuck with me. "What did you just say?"

"Your mug is everywhere?"

"Yes, that's it!"

The muse took me by the hand and led me to my office when a bit of reality snuck into my head. I ran to catch Danny.

"Danny, whatever you do, don't fix the webcam…"

Chapter Eleven. Bob

Alexa! Play Bruce Springsteen's Thunder Road!

I love my Amazon Echo. Best invention ever. Imagine a woman doing what I ask her to do! Never in my lifetime did I ever expect that…

I then opened my laptop.

"Damn webcam!" It's been down a couple of days now. I have no idea how America made out. Oh, I've checked the internet for answers, and there was some BS story about a filmmaker and a mechanical shark. When will people realize their internet hoax stories are just stupid?

I've told a couple of friends about the whole America scenario. They think I'm crazy that I've been daydreaming about a place and a girl 650 miles away. They want to know when I will be coming back to reality. Here's the thing; I'm in reality. Just not their version of it.

Don't think for a minute that I don't hear the whispers. Bob's wife has been gone for three years and now he is behaving like a teenager. The hell with them all. They live their lives as "sheeple." Well, I'm tired of it. I'm tired of being a mindless drone and it's time to make some changes. And those changes start with a trip to the Outer Banks. I've got a bunch of vacation time. I haven't gone or done anything in the last three years. It's all accrued during that time. So why not?

Will it be a temporary or a permanent trip? I don't know. That doesn't need to be decided right now. Right now it's time to throw caution to the wind and just go. Go and live my life. Again.

It's an impromptu decision I know. It's exciting and scary all at the same time. But the decision has been made and there is so much I need to do before I can leave. It was at this moment that the last line of the Springsteen song filled my room.

"It's a town full of losers, I'm pulling out of here to win!"

I chuckled slightly and decided to use that as my mantra going forward....

Chapter Twelve. Charlie

"I reckon you should say yeah," said Danny.

"I am not saying yes."

"Think of all the publicity you could git for the restaurant. Reckon it would be amazin'."

Danny had a point but I am not the type of person who likes to flaunt myself around on TV. I don't even like webcams. I don't know. I don't possibly see how this could help. Although the situation at hand goes deeper than Danny can imagine.

There was a knock at the door. Danny peered out the window. "That feller's back," he said.

I gave him a puzzled look. "We are a restaurant. We have a lot of "fellers" come through here."

He flipped me off. "No, it's the feller with the old man flip-flops," he said.

I felt my stomach drop. "I'm not answering it."

"We're a restaurant, 'member?. You can't NOT open it," said Danny.

"Yeah, but we are a closed restaurant. I don't have to do anything."

The turd wagon outside knocked again. "I can hear you in there," he shouted.

"I don't reckon he's goin' away," said Danny.

I poured some coffee into a mug, though I feared I would need something stronger to get through this conversation. I opened the door. "What do you want?" I said.

"Good morning to you, too. Have you thought anymore about our last conversation?" He could not be more smug.

"How are those fallen arches doing, douche bag?"

"I'm serious," he said. "You have two options, you can sell or you can somehow come up with the money for this rat hole."

I raised the coffee mug to my lips and took a long sip. FORK OFF. That's what the mug said. He looked at me and looked at the ground. I would say that he looked at his shoes but I can't possibly see how he could look at those things. Even glancing hurts my eyes. He looked up again and caught the coffee mug.

"Real mature," he said. "Let me know when you realize you can't afford this place. By the way, nice show on the news the other night. This place will be gone before you know it."

That guy is incredible. Even after he leaves I can still smell his cologne. He lingers and not in a good way.

"What were that all 'bout?" said Danny.

"Nothing."

Danny shook his head. "You're the worst at hidin' stuff. You might as well tell me."

"There is nothing to tell."

I walked back to my office. Maybe Danny had a point. Maybe doing an interview or something would help business. But I have to do it my own way.

Chapter Thirteen. Bob

 With the stand up paddleboard strapped to the roof of the Jeep and Bruno in the back seat in his carrier, I find myself saying out loud to no one, "I can't believe I'm doing this." This is crazy!" as I pull off the Pennsylvania Turnpike at Breezewood and make my way further south. South towards the Outer Banks.

"Lot's of decisions to be made," my self-dialogue continued. But none more immediate than whether I continue onto Washington DC and take the 495 Beltway to 95 towards Fredericksburg, or hop off in Maryland and take the "back way." Less miles, but more time, taking the back way, but potentially more traffic going the other.

I glanced at my watch, the watch Linda got me for my last birthday before she died. Ten am, which puts me in the DC area about noon. Won't be rush hour, I'll take my chances on the Beltway.

I got a very early start out of Cleveland this morning, somewhere around 6 am or so. Sleep did not come easy last night. Was this the beginning of a new life for me, or is this just a temporary adventure? I had no way of knowing at this moment. I had been listening to 92.3 The Fan, the sports talk radio station in Cleveland on the Tune in app on my cell phone, which was plugged into my car's sound system. But as this new chapter starts to unfold for me I only thought it fitting to flip the radio over to 99.1 The Sound, "The Station for Music Discovery on the Outer Banks." John Harper, the best-known DJ, not only on that station, but on the entire beach, just started his air-shift. I used to listen to John each midday at my desk while staring at the Nags Head pier webcam. Now, I may turn into a neighbor of his, who, before now, was only just a voice on the radio.

As the station came to life on the app, Portugal The Man's "Feel It Still" was playing.

"Ooh woo, I'm a rebel just for kicks, now
I've been feeling it since 1966, now
Might be over but I feel it still….."

"Goodbye Cleveland! Hello new life!" I shouted as towns clicked past in the rear view mirror of my Jeep. Gaithersburg, Frederick, DC, Richmond, Newport News, Norfolk, Chesapeake until finally, the sign came into view that I've waited over 9 hours to see, "Welcome to North Carolina."

That's it, there's no turning back now…

Chapter Fourteen. Charlie

I decided to embrace the whole "shark attack" thing –
there really wasn't another option. I could fight it or just
go with it. I decided to go with it; the best way to do that
was to have a shark party. I was up all night making
posters and invitations for the party and had spent most of
the morning hanging them and handing them out.

> **What**: I Survived a Shark Attack Party
> **Where**: Chucks Grub & Tiki Hut
> **When**: Tonight from 6:00pm - ????

I was almost done hanging up the party posters along the
pier when I heard a voice from behind say "I think you
dropped one."

I turned to see a stocky guy in a beret walking toward me.
He handed me the poster. "I'm Ollie." He held out his
hand.

"As in Ollie Frakingham?"

"It's FARKingham, but yes," he said. "And you're
Charlie?"

"Yep. Charlie Foster."

I had to throw Foster in there. I didn't want to become Cher and only have one name. I didn't want to be just Chuck or just Charlie. I love Cher but the only thing we have in common is the desire to turn back time…and amazing cheekbones.

"I've been wanting to talk to you," he said. "Funny I should run into you here."

"Yes, it's incredibly strange that I would be anywhere near my restaurant."

"I want you in my movie," he said.

"No." I started to walk away.

"Just hear me out."

"Fine." I turned around impatiently, wishing I had the FORK OFF coffee mug in my hands. It is so useful in so many situations. Very versatile.

"I want to use the footage from the shark incident. I'll keep it tasteful."

"Why should I trust you?"

"I guess you have no reason to…but technically, I did save your life. Or at least the shark did. Kind of," he said.

"Yeah, I'm not sure attacking me with a mechanical shark is considered saving me."

Ollie fumbled for a moment. "Well, uh, I did my best to help you."

"True." Although I wasn't sure if I really believed it.

"So you'll do it?" He asked.

"I need to think about it."

"I'll do anything," he begged.

"Really? Anything?"

Chapter Fifteen. Party Time (Charlie)

"I want to thank everyone for coming out tonight. It has been a crazy couple of days. I cannot tell you how much it means to feel the love and support of the community tonight. Enjoy yourselves. I love you guys!"

I stepped down off the bar when I remembered, "One more thing. We have a new addition to Chuck's, compliments of Ollie Frakingham-"

"It's Farkingham!"

"Yeah. Anyway, I will be choosing one lucky person for the unveiling tonight. I also have coffee mugs for sale that says WHAT THE FRAK? I SURVIVED A SHARK ATTACK! Get excited!"

Danny started the Jukebox. Jimmy Buffett "FINS" came over the speakers. This could not be any more perfect. A new beginning. A fresh start. And orthopedic flip-flops. What is it with the orthopedic flip-flops?

"Hey, Danny. Do you know who that guy is over there?"

"Which guy?"

"The one in the orthopedic flip-flops."

"Nope, don't reckon I do." He said.

He sat alone drinking a corona, bobbing his head to the music. I decided to find out his deal.

"You new around here?," I said to him.

He stared at me for second, almost like he forgot to speak.

"I'm Bob. Not the sausage."

"Hi Bob, not the sausage."

"GUY."

"Huh?"

"Not the sausage guy."

I smiled and motioned for Bob to follow me. I walked up to the front of the bar. I signaled for Danny to turn the music down.

"Hey everyone, I want you to meet a new friend of mine. Bob Not The Sausage. I think it's time to unveil the new addition to Chucks! Danny drum roll please…"

I pulled the sheet away to reveal a mechanical shark.

"Bob, I want you to be the first to ride it! Cheer for Bob!"

Everyone started chanting: "BOB! BOB! BOB!BOB! BOB!"

I smiled at Bob and whispered in his ear, "Do it for me."

Chapter Sixteen. Bob

"I'd do anything for you America." I muttered.

"My, you're a patriotic one, aren't you? Charlie replied.

"Huh?"

Charlie continued, "you just said you'd do anything for America. You're kinda strange Sausage Guy."

"Oh yeah. Inside joke."

"Must be very inside."

"Yeah. I guess it is," I responded.

So here I was. Here, too was America. She's looking at me. I'm looking at her. Up until this very moment, it had only been me doing the looking. And immediately after thinking that, I realized just how creepy that must sound. But, if I pull this off, America will obviously be very grateful to me.

I made my way to the mechanical shark, and as gracefully as possible, I climbed on top of it. Truth be told, even without the anticipated gyrations of the shark, the room was already spinning. That will happen when you have a few Coronas too many while trying to muster up enough courage to utter even a single word to a girl who you've not yet met, but was the reason for your recent 10-hour car ride.

It was at this point that the last few notes of Jimmy Buffett's "Fins" were finishing on the jukebox. For a second, silence. Until the "Theme to Jaws" kicked in at an ear-splitting level. Lights all around the Tiki Bar started flashing like it was a disco. The music getting louder… LOUDER! And then I felt the whirring of the mechanical shark kick in beneath me as I frantically grabbed onto the dorsal fin/handle. First it bucked forward. Then backwards. To the right. Forward again. Left. Back. Right. Forward. Left……

The last thing I remembered, I threw up all over Ollie Farkingham as the shark sent me airborne, and crashing into the bar. I also took out 3 or 4 tourists who seemed to be enjoying the spectacle up until that point….

Chapter Seventeen. Charlie

For the first time in a long time, a guy slept over. Granted, he passed out and doesn't realize he slept over, but still, he slept over.

Such an odd way to make an introduction. I feel somewhat responsible for the guy. After all, I did make him climb on the shark. Climb on the shark. That is definitely a phrase for a coffee mug. I should at least give him a t-shirt or something.

The place is a mess. Thank God for being closed on Sundays.

I could hear Danny in the other room. Great. Two guys slept over.

"Good morning, sunshine."

Danny roused awake, squinting as if the light was painful to look at. "I'll put some coffee on," I said as I walked into the kitchen.

I pulled the filters out and started making my special breakfast blend. Today calls for the finest. I got the grinder out for the coffee beans. I love the smell of fresh coffee in the morning. As I turned the grinder on I heard the groans of two grown men.

"Sorry, guys! It will be worth it, I promise."

Danny managed to make his way into the kitchen.

"The coffee is almost ready," I said.

He held his hand up as if to say that it was okay. I high fived him instead.

"Ouch!"

"You're such a little girl," I told him.

"Speakin' of lil' girl, who is that sleeping beauty over yonder?"

"Bob Evans, I guess."

"Reckon he gave you a fake name, if you ask me," said Danny.

"I don't know. Maybe. I guess I kind of deserved a fake name. I didn't know he had an inner ear problem when I basically forced him on the shark."

"Inner ear problem? Nah, that be called too much Corona."

We both laughed a little but were interrupted by a knock on the door. I poured some coffee and went to answer the door. Oh great. The turd wagon from the county. I could see his turd head through the window. Reluctantly, I walked over and brilliantly tripped over a lost flip-flop. I picked it up instinctively.

"It's Sunday. We're closed."

I started to shut the door. He put his hand up to stop it from closing.

"We need to talk, Charlie," he said.

I slapped him in the forehead with the flip-flop. He looked at me stunned.

"Bug," I said. "It's gone."

He rubbed his forehead with his hand almost looking perplexed.

"I'm guessing that's a common look for you," I told him.

"I see you've started wearing orthopedic flip-flops," he said pointing to the shoe in my hand.

"They're not mine," I said. "If I were you I would wash that bug off your forehead."

He started to walk in as if to use the restaurant bathrooms. I shoved him back outside. "We're closed," I said, as I slammed the door in his face. That felt good.

Just then Danny came around the corner, "What's all the fussin' goin' on?"

"Shoes," I said. "I think it's time to wake up Cinderella."

I walked into the kitchen and poured him some coffee. Bob started to rouse awake as I walked toward him.

"Good morning," I said.

"Where am I?"

"You're at my restaurant. I also live upstairs so technically you are at my house, I guess."

I handed him the coffee. He took a sip and got a puzzled look on his face. "Where's my flip-flop?"

"Oh yeah, it's right here." I handed him the flip-flop. "Not quite how that played out in Cinderella."

Bob managed a grin.

"Let me make you some breakfast."

Chapter Eighteen. Bob

"Great, I'm so hungry I can eat a horse. Just please don't make any Bob Evans sausage for me, for you know, obvious reasons."

"Yeah, about that. That really your name? Danny, my maintenance guy and I were just talking about it. Figured you were so drunk you just came up with an alias, to protect the innocent, as they say."

"I wish I did. Besides, if I were to come up with a fake name, I'd like to think I could be more creative than Bob Evans."

"Yeah, I reckon you would. Now here, take your orthopedic flip-flop and let me finish making breakfast."

With that, Charlie went back into to the kitchen. Figuring I could be some help, or at least not have to drink my coffee alone, I followed her in.

"Hey America......., or I'm sorry, I don't think I actually know your name."

"Yeah, you called me America last night too. What's up with that?"

"Um.....well, uh, nothing, never mind. Just the Corona talking."

"Yeah, well, the name is Charlie. Nice to formally meet you, Not the Sausage Guy."

"Bob. Just call me Bob."

"Ok Bob. Tell me, what's the deal with orthopedic flip-flops? You're not the first I've seen wearing them. Some other turd wagon showed up here recently wearing them. It's not a style I've ever seen before. Likely not one I'll ever want to see again either."

"Well, it is the wave of the future for beach footwear!" It was at this moment I realized I didn't work for that horrible company anymore and mustered out "I know, pretty ridiculous idea. I can't believe I gave so much of my life to that place, selling these awful things."

Charlie finished making breakfast and as I sat down to eat, it occurred to me that one thing America, I mean Charlie, knew how to do, you know, besides looking cute, is to make a killer meal. Scrambled eggs made with cheddar cheese and diced ham, crab and onions. Sausage gravy and biscuits, hash browns and more of that wonderful smelling coffee. The perfect hangover remedy. I ate like I hadn't eaten in 24 hours. And I hadn't. Must have been why the Coronas affected me the way they did. I ended up having to wobble away from the table.

The company at breakfast would have been much, much better if that maintenance guy wasn't around. Why was he here anyway? It didn't appear that he and Charlie were involved with each other at all. Maybe she felt like she needed a chaperone since she had a stranger, a guy who she thought had given her a fake name, staying the night. Not by anyone's choice however, other than that of the importer of Corona beer and the maker of that damn mechanical shark. That is one "carnival" ride I will not ever get on again.

"Charlie! Wonderful breakfast! But, I don't want to wear out my welcome…"

"Too late for that Sausage Guy…"

"I don't blame you for feeling like that. If you don't mind, before leaving I really would like to have a seat on the pier and enjoy the ocean a bit."

"Reckon I can't stop you," Charlie replied.

I walked out onto the Nags Head pier. Everything was in place just as I was accustomed to seeing it on the webcam. The red, pink and yellow colored picnic tables. The tables and chairs for Chuck's Grub & Tiki Bar. The Atlantic Ocean. There were fishermen out at the end of the pier too. I took a seat along the rail, facing east towards the water and watched the waves roll in. I breathed in the sea air. I reveled in the sea breeze and my soul felt at peace. Like I was at home. A home, that up until now, I didn't even know existed.

After an hour or so of taking in the sounds and the sights. The mesmerizing sound of waves crashing, one at a time on the beach behind me. Dolphins, 50 yards offshore playfully heading south towards Hatteras Island. The seagulls following them, occasionally dive bombing, picking up scraps of food left behind. I unsteadily regained my feet and made my way back inside to Chuck's, still feeling the effects of the Corona and from being thrown from that damn mechanical shark.

"Charlie, I know you're closed today and I want to get out of your hair. But I don't think I'm able to drive yet."

"Well, call Roy's Taxi to take you to where you need to go. I need to clean this place up. Today's my only day off this week and I don't need to spend it babysitting you."

"I tried Roy's. Apparently he's taking someone up to the airport in Norfolk and won't be back for a couple of hours. I tried calling my cousin too, who I'm staying with in Manteo, but his phone seems to be off. Goes straight to voicemail."

(Sigh) "Alright, where does your cousin live in Manteo? I guess I can run you there. Then you and your cousin can come back and pick up your car later. I have to run Danny home to Wanchese anyway."

"He's on Eleanor Dare Place, about a block north of downtown, over by the cemetery."

Charlie yelled out, "Hey Danny, let's go! I also have to take sausage guy to his cousin's over on the island. The sooner I get rid of the two of you, the sooner I can get on with my day."

A few seconds later, the three of us jumped into Charlie's Jeep. The Jeep was black, it had no top nor doors. A real surf vehicle here on the Outer Banks. I squeezed into the tiny backseat because that putz Danny yelled "shotgun!" Damn, I already don't like him. Charlie put the Jeep into gear and turned left out of the pier parking lot and drove down Virginia Dare Trail, locally referred to as simply, "the Beach Road."

The Beach Road, runs parallel to what is called the 158 Bypass. The main highway running the length of the northern beaches which includes Kitty Hawk, Kill Devil Hills, and here in Nags Head. The speed limit on the Beach Road is 35, compared to the 55 MPH speed limit on the Bypass. The Beach Road is much more scenic and often quicker getting you to your destination since there are fewer traffic lights. Unfortunately, because of the wind noise, I couldn't carry on a conversation with Charlie and Danny. I just sat in the back and enjoyed the ride.

Charlie's Jeep made its way to Whalebone Junction and started for the Manteo-Nags Head Causeway, the only way to get onto Roanoke Island from the beach by car. Basically, the island consists of two towns, Wanchese on the south side; Manteo on the north. As we continued down the causeway we passed Sugar Creek on the right, The Tale of The Whale, and Senator Marc Basnight's Lone Cedar on the left. All three restaurants serving up excellent local seafood. I made a mental note that maybe I could take Charlie for dinner at one of them this week.

As we crossed the Washington Baum Bridge over Roanoke Sound, the sun, high overhead, sparkled off the ripples of water. Like diamonds dancing. Boats were making their way out of Pirates Cove Marina and under the bridge off to a day of chasing fish.

At the Manteo-Wanchese junction, Charlie surprised me and took the left in the direction of Wanchese. She was going to drop off Danny first! Apparently, she didn't feel threatened being alone with me in the Jeep. That's a start......

Charlie handled the curves down Route 345 towards Wanchese like she's driven them all her life. In fact, she had, having been born and raised in the little fishing village before taking over Chuck's Grub & Tiki Bar on the beach.

About four miles from the turn off at the junction, Charlie pulled left into a gravel driveway. At the end of the drive was a boat on a trailer that had seen better days. The wheels of the trailer slowly sinking into the earth beneath it. Paint peeling off the wooden boat. It appears that it hasn't been sea-worthy for a quite a while. Behind the boat and off slightly to the right, was a white, with black trim, double-wide mobile home. A North Carolina flag flying proudly outside the front door.

"Here you go Danny." Charlie said.

"Yep, home sweet doublewide," Danny replied.

"Now don't you be late for work tomorrow. I'm thinking about pulling that mechanical shark out of the bar and I'll need your help. Too much potential liability, as our friend in the back seat here demonstrated so brilliantly last night."

I smiled sheepishly.

"Don't worry boss. I'll have the old lady drive me in tomorrow when she's headin' to the bait store."

With that Danny jumped out of the Jeep and scampered up the four steps to the doublewide. As he opened the screen door he was immediately met with the sound of a woman yelling at him. No doubt for not having come home last night. What she was saying, however, was lost due to a dog barking incessantly in the background.

I jumped into the shotgun seat, relieved to be able to stretch my legs out a bit as Charlie muttered, almost under her breath, "Come on cowboy, let's get you to your cousin's so I can finally enjoy my day."

We drove the four miles back to the junction and continued into the town of Manteo. Mostly we rode in silence. Charlie turned right on Devon Street, drove past the cemetery on the left. A block down further she turned left onto Eleanor Dare Place. My cousin's house was the only one built on stilts and was the newest on the street. Charlie pulled into the driveway. As she did, she said, "I always wondered who lived here. I figured it had to be some rich dude."

"I don't know about rich," I replied. "I do know that he has a county job of some sort."

As I mostly fell out of the Jeep I both thanked Charlie and apologized for the hassle I have caused.

"No worries Not the Sausage Guy. Hey, I'll be playing my uke down at the Tiki Bar this week if you want to stop out. Just promise you'll behave this time. And if you can't count the number of Coronas you've had, then I will. Bring your cousin too if you like. First round will be on me."

"Thanks. I'm sure we'll do that."

With that, Charlie backed the Jeep back out onto the street and was gone. My cousin's car wasn't there, but I knew he would leave the door open for me.

Still being too unsteady on my feet, I opted to take the elevator located on the outside of the house up to the main living area, rather than trying to climb the steps.

Chapter Nineteen. Charlie

> Strummin' my four string
> On my front porch swing

Jimmy Buffett would probably appreciate it if I didn't steal his song.

Let's see here…
> You got thrown off the shark
> Then everything thing went dark

Kind of a blues feel. I like it..

> I couldn't wait to say goodbye
> My little sausage guy

Yikes. That definitely doesn't sound flattering. Maybe I should stick to some of the classics for tonight.

I looked at the clock and saw I had just enough time to grab a mug and do some painting before the restaurant opened. Usually painting cleared my head, but I couldn't get Bob off my mind. There was something about that guy I couldn't figure out. I'm not sure if it was good or bad. As I finished up I heard Danny come in through the back.

"So want me to get rid of that shark?"

"I don't know. Let's hold off for now. Just make sure no one else can ride it," I said.

Danny shrugged his shoulders. "Whatcha workin' on?"

"Another mug." I turned it so Danny couldn't see what I had painted.

"Nothing special."

"Cool."

Danny left the room and walked into the kitchen, no doubt to get some coffee. I went back to the mug -- I liked it. It made me smile a bit. I came out of my daydream to foot steps. They didn't sound like Danny's heavy steps. These sounded more clickety-clack, clickety-clack. Like flip-flops. Maybe Bob came back for his car.

I hopped out my chair and went to the main dining room. Oh no, I felt my stomach in my throat. Not the turd wagon.

"Get out. You are not welcome here."

"Charlie, you have to talk to me at some point. This is going to happen unless you can come up with the cash."

"There's no way you are getting this place." I grabbed his arm and pushed him toward the door.

"You're dreaming, Charlie."

With that I slammed the door in his face. I turned around to see Danny standing by the bar.

"How much of that did you hear?"

"Enough I reckon. Why didn't you tell me?" He said.

"I'm going to fix it. He is not taking my place."

Danny took a step toward me and I fell into his arms. "I don't know what I am going to do. He won't leave me alone. I have to figure it out."

Danny held me tight. At first it was reassuring then it got weird.

"All right, I think we are done here. Thanks, Daniel."

The rest of the day was pretty quiet. Danny and I were both in deep thought. We had to save the restaurant somehow. I went through the motions of serving customer after customer until I saw Bob walk through the door. The site of him was a welcome one. His smile. His dumb orthopedic flip-flops. I gave a quick wave and ran back to my studio to grab the mug I made earlier. Bob was standing at the bar when I came back in.

"Corona?"

Bob shrugged his shoulders, "sure."

I handed him a coffee mug full of corona. He examined it as he took it from my hands. He smiled. "It says 'Not The Sausage.'"

"Yeah, I figured you would have less explaining to do. Have fun tonight but beware of the shark." I punched him as I headed to the mic with my ukulele.

Chapter Twenty. Bob

After getting back to my cousin's yesterday I decided to take it easy after my "wild night" at Chuck's Tiki Bar. I took a bit of a nap, then I sat out at his back yard pool trying to get some coloring in my pasty, white northern skin. I didn't want to overdo it. I didn't want to look like a typical tourist. You know, the kind, that spend their entire first day in the sun and their second and third days anywhere but in the sun as they nurse their sunburn back to an acceptable threshold of pain. No. For whatever reason, I was trying to fit in with the locals. I didn't know why. I was a tourist. Maybe it had something to do with my notion of moving down here and adopting the "island life" myself.

As it turned out, I did get a bit more pink than I had intended. So I hoofed it down to the Piggly Wiggly near the Chesley Mall to grab a bottle of aloe. The salt air and the pool soothes my soul. Now it was time to soothe my burning skin.

After applying a liberal amount of aloe on my face and shoulders, I called Roy's Taxi to bring me back to the pier since my car was still parked there. My cousin has been strangely busy the last two days and wasn't able to help me retrieve it. When I mentioned bringing me to the pier he mumbled something and appeared none to happy about it as he walked away.

And now I find myself back at Chuck's Tiki Bar with a cold Corona in my hand…..well, in my new "Not the Sausage" mug as America, I mean Charlie, took to the stage.

It was a bit weird watching her up in there in the spotlight of the stage. One minute she's slinging drinks and the next she's banging on that ukulele. First time I ever saw a woman playing a uke. She had a name for it too. I think she called it Duke. Duke the Uke is what it was. Before launching into James Taylor's "Carolina in My Mind" she explained that if B.B. King could name his guitar, Lucille, then she saw no reason why her instrument shouldn't also have a name.

I sat there slowly sipping on my Corona listening. I told myself that tonight I would take my time and pace myself. No need for a replay of two nights ago. As Charlie launched into Bob Seger's "Old Time Rock and Roll," a text on my cell phone chirped.

"Hey cuz. I'm free now. Where you be?"

It was my cousin Joe. He did mention maybe getting together for dinner or a beer tonight. He said maybe Fish Heads down at the Outer Banks Pier, but nothing was ever confirmed.

"I'm at Chuck's Tiki Bar on the Nags Head Pier."

"Again?!?!?!"

"Yes, again. Why you don't like this place?"

"It's not that. It's just.....oh long story. Is that owner girl there tonight?"

"You mean Charlie? Yeah she's here. Why?"

"I need to talk to her, but its been hard to pin her down. You gonna be there awhile?"

It was at this point I saw Charlie look down from the stage at me and frown. No doubt a bit upset that I've been texting with my cousin and not listening to her. As she started into "Brilliant Disguise" by Bruce Springsteen, I quickly typed into my phone, "yes I'll be here a while. Charlie is performing onstage now and I want to stop texting and listen."

"Ok cuz. Sorry. I'll join you down there in a bit."

Charlie had this smokiness to her voice when she sang. It wasn't there when she talked, but it was definitely an alluring quality. I sat there for almost a half hour listening to her go from one great song into the next. When all of a sudden.....WHACK!

Someone smacked me on the back. And I mean HARD. I turned expecting to see someone pissed off at me for something I did the other night when I got a little unruly. I do recall having thrown up on some people. But it was just little old Danny. Apparently since we had breakfast the other morning and Charlie and I dropped him off at his trailer in Wanchese, now we're some sort of best of friends.

"What the hell Danny! What was that for?"

"Oh, nothing. Just thought I'd come over and say howdy."
"New mug I see. Must have been the one Charlie was working on earlier."

"Yeah, I guess. I don't know."

Danny took a quick glance around, almost like he wanted to make sure no one would hear what he would say next, "how did Charlie seem to you when you got here?"

"Fine I guess. Why?"

"I don't know." Danny said, his eyes still darting around the room. "Just seemed like Charlie was spooked about somethin' earlier. Something she said she needed to handle. I never really saw her like that before."

"Well Danny. I haven't known Charlie that long." While saying those words, I had to smile to myself as I thought back to all those months of actually watching her before actually meeting her just a couple of nights ago. "So I don't really know if she was off kilter at all."

"Yeah. Gotcha Sausage Guy. I reckon you wouldn't. Hey, how about another beer?"

"Yeah. Thanks Danny. But here, let me pay for one for you too."

As Charlie segued into Free Bird, Danny said, "Thanks Hoss! I'll go grab a couple and be right back."

"…..And this bird you cannot change
Lord knows I can't change…..
Won't you fly high Free Bird, yeah….."

Charlie belted out the song with a huge smile on her face. Obviously she loves this part of her job I thought….

At the moment that Charlie closed her eyes and went into her Free Bird uke solo and Danny left to go grab our beers, my cousin Joe made his way into Chuck's and sat down at the table next me. That was when all hell broke loose!

First I heard the sound of glass crashing on the ground. Danny was returning to our table with the two beers when he dropped them. Cold Corona beer and glass flying everywhere around my feet. Then from stage Charlie broke from her song and yelled "YOU! Turd wagon! You get out of my bar and don't you ever come back!"

I looked around to see who Charlie was directing her venom toward, but it appeared she was looking right at me and my cousin! Not knowing exactly what was going on, I was bewildered when I saw Joe approach the stage apparently trying to reason with Charlie.

"Come on Charlie. You know you need to talk to me about this. You can't keep avoiding me. I'm telling this for your own good. Honestly!"

"Don't you ever come in here and interrupt my customers again" Charlie screamed as spittle appeared around the corners of her mouth. "And you!" She said now looking at me. "You! You're in on this too! I should have figured, the way you're both walking around in those ridiculous orthopedic flip-flops. How was I that dumb? Both of you get out! I don't ever want to see either of you again.

With that Charlie left the stage and went running back towards her studio and slammed the door shut behind her shouting as she ran "Concert is over!"

Chapter Twenty-One. Charlie

"Concert is over!"

I slammed the door shut behind me. How did I not see this? The dumb orthopedic flip-flops. The mysterious cousin who works for the county. I mean, I even made a mug for him. And it was a nice mug. I wasn't even trying to be mean.

Just then, Danny opened the door. "What was that all about?"

I debated on telling him it was just my time of the month and that I needed chocolate or something. I knew that he would see through it. "I feel like a fool."

"Because you lost your shit in front of everyone!"

"Oh my gosh! No wonder Maggie always yells at you."

That was a low blow, even for me. Danny lowered his eyes and looked at his feet.

"I'm sorry, Danny. You know I didn't mean it. I'm just upset."

"Really?" His sarcastic tone left nothing to the imagination. We both laughed out of awkwardness.

"I'm gonna lose this place, Danny. That turd wagon out there is trying to steal this place out from under me."

"I don't reckon I understand. You own this place, dontcha?"

"I lease the building but not the pier. I have to buy the pier if I want to stay."

"Oh."

"Are they still here?"

"Who?"

"The turd wagon brothers."

Danny turned and cracked the door open to check the dining room, "yep."

I grabbed two mugs from my desk, painted a few quick words on them, and marched my little butt out the door. There they were sitting as smug as can be in their stupid little flip-flops. I could barely stand the sight of them.

"All right, turd wagon. You want to talk? Follow me."

He looked shocked. He rose from the table and followed me. "It's about time," he said.

We walked over to the corner of the room, by the shark. The turd wagon looked at it for a second. "This must be the shark Bob was telling me about."

"How nice. Get on if you want to talk."

"I'm not getting on that thing."

"That thing has a name. It's Lester. And you'll get on if you want to talk."

"I can't believe I'm doing this. Just don't actually turn it on. I have an inner ear thing."

This could not be more perfect. I gestured for him to get on Lester. He climbed on and settled in…as much as you can on a mechanical shark. "Now let's talk," he said.

I giggled to myself and flipped the switch on the shark. "Good luck with that."

Lester tossed him all over the place. He lasted longer than I thought. When he landed on the ground, I walked over to him. Bob was already by the his side, helping him up. "Here's a parting gift for you two love birds."

I handed them the mugs. They each read: GET OUT.

I opened the door and gestured for them to get on the other side of it. Bob seemed confused as they left. The turd wagon fell down three times in the parking lot. I don't think he was lying about that inner ear problem. Must run in the family.

Chapter Twenty-Two. Bob

"Looks like we're leaving my car here this time" Joe sputtered as I picked him up from the pavement for the third time in the pier parking lot.

"What was all that about?" I wanted to know.

"Oh, that bitch, she doesn't know what she's up against."

"Come on now Joe. She may have sent you head over heels on that mechanical shark in there, but Charlie is not a bitch."

"Hard to tell by me" Joe responded as his knees buckled yet again at the car door.

I propped Joe up against the car, my body holding him in place as I opened the passenger side door. I carefully helped him into his seat and finally got him buckled in. I got in and put my Jeep into first gear as we drove south on the Beach Road to the Manteo – Nags Head Causeway and back to Joe's place on Eleanor Dare Place. Mostly we drove in silence with Joe occasionally holding his head and moaning. At one point, just as we passed Pirate's Cove and just before the Manteo turn-off, I thought he was gonna hurl. Thankfully he didn't. The last thing I wanted to worry about on this trip was cleaning my cousin's puke out of my car.

Once home I got Joe upstairs, again using the elevator on the side of the house. He shook off his flip-flops and laid down on the couch. I always thought it strange that with all his money, Joe's furniture was made of "pleather." That hybrid of leather and plastic. Certainly he can afford real leather. Pleather is horrible in the summer. You sweat and stick to the furniture. Leaving behind a pool of sweat on the cushions as you got up.

"So Joe, you want to tell me what's going on?" I said, choosing my words as carefully as I could. "I was having a perfectly good time and then you come in and bust the place up."

"I didn't bust nothin' up!" Joe spit back.

"Well, maybe not literally, but you didn't just ruin my night, you also ruined Charlie's and everyone else's trying to enjoy a relaxing evening."

"Look" Joe said, while still holding his head in his hands. "Charlie's evening might have been ruined, but I'm telling you, if she doesn't talk to me like a grown up, and I mean soon, its her life that's going to be ruined. She doesn't realize it, but I'm not the bad guy here. I'm the guy trying to help her."

"Help her with what exactly?"

Now it was Joe's turn to be cautious with his words. Almost like he didn't know what he could say and not say. After all, I had struck up somewhat of a friendship with Charlie these past few days. "Well, Charlie owns the Tiki Bar on the pier, but she doesn't own the pier itself." Joe started explaining, "The local Nags Head family that owns the pier is in negotiations to sell the pier to the county. The county wants to use the space where Charlie's Tiki Bar sits for more educational purposes than beer, crab cakes and ukulele music. They want to take advantage of the popularity of the state run aquarium here on Roanoke Island by opening a small tidal pool and museum/gift shop in that space."

"So what does that mean for Charlie?" I asked.

"The reason I want to talk to her is because even though I work for the county, I'm friends with the current owners of the pier and they think it's only fair that Charlie not be thrown out into the street. They want to find some resolution."

"So you're not really talking to her as a warrant of the county then?"

"No, of course not. That is not even in my department. I don't deal with those things. I mostly deal with dog and bike licenses. Mundane things like that."

For the first time it dawned on me that Joe wasn't quite the big shot as I thought he was. As he led others to believe, including his own parents; my aunt and uncle. I asked, "Does Charlie know that?"

"I don't know, I don't think so. She never lets me get far enough into the conversation to tell her I'm there more as a representative of the pier owners and not the county."

"What would the owners of the pier think would be a fair resolution?"

Joe slowly and unsteadily pulled himself up from the couch and went to the kitchen to grab two Red Stripe beers. Watching him wobble on his way to the refrigerator made my head hurt. He opened both beers and handed me one. He took a long pull from his before answering. Finally after reflecting for a few moments Joe said, "I think the best thing for Charlie is if she buys the pier herself before the county's negotiations are completed."

"How can she do that? Aren't the negotiations already in progress?"

"That's the beauty of it cuz" Joe explained. "The negotiations just got started and lucky for Charlie, nothing ever moves quickly when it comes to the county government."

"What is the county willing to pay for the pier?" I wanted to know.

"Ah, now that's the sticky wicket," Joe said. "As an employee of the county, I can't divulge that number. But I think if she approached the owners, they would open the door to talking."

"I don't know Charlie that well," I continued, "but I can't imagine she would have that kind of money."

"She doesn't need to do this on her own cuz. I know people willing to partner up with her to help buy it. And those people would be more than willing to keep Chuck's Tiki Bar in place. These are investors and they see the value in a bar and restaurant over a tidal pool and museum – gift shop. For one, the Tiki Bar brings in money all year round. It's not just tourists like you that go there, but in the off season a fair many of the locals go there too. I suspect the museum and tidal pool would do alright during the season, but would be a ghost town after the tourists go home."

"Good point."

"Charlie needs to sit down and listen to me. She really can make this all work to her advantage."

"Joe, I'll tell you what. Let's give her tonight to simmer back down and tomorrow give me a crack at talking to her."

Joe agreed, and with that, we finished off our Red Stripes and said our good nights as we went off to our individual bedrooms.

Chapter Twenty-Three. Charlie

I woke up with a renewed sense of self. Ready to take on the day. Ready to take on the county. I grabbed my paddleboard, high fived Lester, the mechanical shark, and headed to the ocean. She was calm this morning. My board hit the water and I was free.

A few people were out by the pier. A few with their dogs. A few with their kids. These are the days I feel lucky. I have a successful restaurant. I have good friends. I don't want to be anywhere else.

Just as I was really feeling centered, I heard someone yell, "Hey, it's the shark lady from the video!"

I snapped out of my happy place to see a few kids staring and pointing. I felt a twitch in my middle finger but remembered I was supposed to be embracing this. "Yep, that's me."

They gave a me a thumbs up, "That was gnarly, dude."

I paddled to shore. It was time to head in anyway. "Can we get a picture?"

"Sure."

The kids took the picture and went on their merry way. I went inside to shower. It was perhaps the best shower I had in a long time. The ocean water had been just cold enough that the warmth of the shower made me not want to leave. The smell of coffee wafted up. Wait, what? Who in the world is here?

I dried off and followed the smell of coffee. I had a donut in one hand and a bat in the other. I was feeling hungry and aggressive. I turned the corner to see Danny.

"What are you doing here so early?"

"Fixin' the webcam."

I punched him in the arm, "Seriously, I hate you."

I grabbed a cup of coffee. "Want to come?" I motioned toward the beach. "I think I'm gonna take a walk before we open."

Danny grabbed a cup and followed. "So what the hell happened last night? You lost your shit."

"I need to figure this thing out. And Bob…"

"You totally ruined my free beer dude. Sausage Guy was paying."

"Danny, all your beers are free."

"I know, but you killed the vibe."

"You mean the turd wagon and Bob killed the vibe. I can't believe I didn't see it sooner. He's been in on this thing the whole time."

"You don't know for sure, Chuck."

"Pretty sure I do. The orthopedic flip-flops should have tipped me off."

"Why do them things bother you so much?"

"They're orthopedic flip-flops!! That's so dumb."

"You ever worn a pair?"

"Umm, no."

"I reckon you should give 'em a chance, Chuck."

"The flip-flops or Bob?"

"Both I reckon."

"I don't know, Danny. I have pretty solid arches."

Danny shoved me and I lost my footing for a moment. The rest of the walk was silent except for the sound of the water and the seagulls. I mainly looked at my feet, which made me think of flip-flops, which made me think of Bob. I don't know what to think. Maybe he was just an innocent bystander. But maybe he wasn't. Danny interrupted my thought process.

"Looky there Chuck. You see what I'm seein'?"

I looked up toward the restaurant to see Bob standing with the turd wagon. I turned to Danny. "I'm not going up there."

Danny grabbed my arm. "Just hear 'em out."

"Why should I?"

"Because at this point, you ain't got shit to lose."

Point taken. I walked up to the restaurant and unlocked the doors.

"You guys want coffee?"

Chapter Twenty-Four. Bob

"Depends, did you poison it?" Joe wanted to know.

"It had crossed my mind." Charlie said, "but no, its fine. You, know, if a little rat poison is fine for your digestion."

Danny spit out the sip of coffee he had just taken and laughingly added, "Charlie's coffee is as bad as rat poison sometimes, but I reckon I'm still standin'."

Charlie glanced sideways at Danny and frowned. A look that Danny no doubt had seen before. "What brings you boys out here?" She asked. "I thought I made it plenty clear last night that neither of you were welcome here."

"Well Charlie," I said with a certain amount of hesitancy, not wanting my head taken off, "I saw you out on the water again on the webcam…"

"Again?!?!? What do you mean again?" Charlie asked as she shot Danny another one of those sideways glances. Poor guy I thought. He must be on the receiving end of those glances a lot.

"I don't know," I stammered. "Look, we need to talk. You're in some trouble but I think we can help you out." I looked over at Joe and asked him to take a walk out to the end of the pier with Danny. "Let me talk alone to Charlie please." I said to the two.

"Fine cuz" added Joe. "If you think you can talk some sense into her, then you go for it. God knows I've tried and haven't been able to."

As Danny and Joe went down the pier where a dozen fishermen were already out trying to catch their lunch, I noticed Charlie giving me one of those glances that up until now had seemed to be reserved for Danny.

"Ok Not the Sausage Guy, you got me alone. What do you have to say?"

"Charlie, as you probably know, my cousin Joe works for the county…."

"Yeah, small place we all kinda know each other's business."

"Well, he told me last night that while you own Chuck's, you don't own the pier. Is that right?"

"Yeah, so?"

"Well, the family that owns the pier is in active negotiations with the county but they don't want you to be left out in the cold on this. The county's plans are to use your space for, well, educational purposes."

"And your cousin is doing the negotiating for the county and wants me out, is that it?"

"No. Not actually. It turns out my cousin isn't anything more than a glorified dog catcher or something for the county. Had the whole family fooled. But that's another story. Anyway, he's actually here on the request of the pier owner. I think if the county knew that he was here, they wouldn't exactly be happy with him."

"So he's not trying to hand me eviction papers then?"

"No. Well, not yet anyway. I think he's trying to avoid all that actually."

"You say he's here as a representative of the owners of the pier and not the county. Does he have a plan? Or is he just giving me a head's up to all this?"

"Honestly, he mentioned last night that you could save yourself by buying the pier. The negotiations with the county were just starting, but nothing with the county moves quickly and that the family might listen to your offer."

"My offer?!?!?!?! Exactly how much money do you idiots think I have anyway? I have this business, I have my Jeep and my stand up board. Not much else. I can't buy the pier! I KNEW talking to you guys was going to be a waste of time!"

"Hold on! I don't know exactly what Joe is thinking but he mentioned knowing some investors that would being willing to purchase the pier with you and keep Chuck's Grub & Tiki Bar in place. They see the business sense in keeping you here."

"Who are these people exactly? Is this all on the up and up?"

"That I can't answer. Those are the details that Joe would have to address. I just wanted to get you alone first to let you know this may not be as bad as you think. But then again….., well, I just don't have specific answers, those will have to come from Joe."

At that moment, out of the corner of my eye I saw Joe and Danny walking back towards us. They seemed to be getting along. Perhaps Joe explained to Danny, while out on the walk all that was going on. Maybe to get an ally from Charlie's side to at least talk some reason to her. As they approached, Charlie simply said, "Joe, let's have that talk you've been wanting to have."

Joe was seemingly surprised by Charlie's invitation to talk and added "No shark this time?"

"No Joe." Charlie laughed, "no shark," as she and Joe walked into the cool of the restaurant leaving Danny and I out on the pier to enjoy the early morning sunshine.

Chapter Twenty-Five. Charlie

I guess Joe isn't the turd wagon I thought…But, he's still a little bit of one.

"So how much money are we talking, Joe?"

"I don't know. We will have to set up some meetings to figure it out. It would have to be a competitive offer, but I think the current owners would cut you some slack," he said.

The reality of the situation was finally sinking in. Ever since the shark attack I had kind of pushed it out of my mind. I knew it was there but I had somehow convinced myself that it wasn't a real threat.

"You're quiet," Joe said. "I'm not used to you being at a loss for words."

"Just thinking," I said. "This is kind of my whole future." I snapped out of it enough to punch him in the arm. "Okay. Get out of here. I have customers coming in."

"I will set up some meetings. Sound good?"

"Yep. Thanks, Joe."

Joe winked as he walked out the door. It was kind of creepy. I took a walk around the dining room to make sure everything was set when I saw Danny and Bob still talking at the bar. "Hey, Ernie and Bert. We're about to open."

Danny flipped me off.

"Watch it, Danny. We have webcams."

He flipped me off again.

"Bob, you want something to eat?"

"Thanks, I should probably get out of here. Joe is waiting by the car."

"Catch ya later, Boob."

"Did you just call me Boob?"

I shrugged my shoulders and flipped over the open sign.

"Maybe."

He flicked my nose as he walked through the door.

"There be some flirting going on 'twixt you and Sausage Guy?" Danny startled me. I had forgotten he was in the room.

"Shut up. You're on the clock."

I could hear Danny muttering something in the background. I didn't really care. For the first time in several weeks, I felt a glimmer of hope. I still had no idea how I would come up with the money, but there was at least hope. With that, I had my first customer of the day.

"Hello, folks. My name is Chuck. Can I get you something to drink while you look over the menu?"

"Are you that shark attack, lady?"

I put my pen and paper down. "Yes. Can I get you something to drink or eat?"

"We are waiting on my cousin."

"Okay, I guess I will come back."

Those are some weird dudes. I went back to the bar to grab some coffee. Looked like the cousin was at the table. I went back over.

"Can I —"

"Chuck, have you hit celebrity status yet?"

It took me a second to get my bearings straight. "What the Frak? Ollie?"

I saw him cringe a little.

"Everyone is loving your scene in the movie. I mean, I've only screened it to a limited audience, but it's great."

I had kind of forgotten about the movie. "So the movie is out? I'm in it?"

"Well yeah, you have the mechanical shark don't you?"

"Yes. Yes, I do."

The door opened. Another group came in to be seated. "I will be right with you."

"Are you the shark lady?"

I looked at Ollie. "Limited audience, huh?

He shrugged his shoulders, "What can I say? You're a hit."

Danny tapped me on the shoulder. "We just got a reservation for 27 people tonight."

"We don't even take reservations."

Danny had a goofy smile, "Reckon we do now."

Ollie butted in, "Looks like everyone wants a piece of the shark lady."

Chapter Twenty-Six. Bob

As we got out to the car and pulled into the traffic onto the Beach Road, we decided to grab a quick beer at the Lucky 12 Tavern and chat. But I couldn't contain myself any further. "Well?" I asked my cousin.

Coyly, Joe replied "Well, what?"

"Come on, don't be a jerk,. You know what…"

"Yeah," Joe said laughing, but judging by the look on his face after looking at the look on my face, I could tell he was afraid to push the joke any further. "I think she understands the necessity of hitting this thing head on. She wants me to set up some meetings with both the current owners of the piers and the group of investors that likely would make a run at buying the place."

"So she's out of the woods then…"

"Well, I wouldn't say that exactly,' Joe said. "Yes, we have a group of investors and while I don't know the figure the owners are looking at wanting, I would guess that Charlie and this investment group is still going to be short in the money department."

"How short?" I asked.

"Again, not knowing exactly what it's going to take, I'm thinking something in the vicinity of about twenty-five grand."

"Yowza! That's a lot of money." Just then we had pulled into the parking lot of Lucky 12. Careful of the large puddle from last night's rain, we stepped out of the car and went into the building. Jamie, the hostess, dressed in cargo shorts, black Converse sneakers and a tie-dyed, Lucky 12 t-shirt, led us to a booth to the left of the bar. Dropping menus and silverware rolled up into paper napkins on the table in front of us, she asked us for our drink order. Nags Head IPA from the Lost Colony Brewery for me, a Carolina Blonde Ale for Joe.

Picking up our conversation where we left off, I asked, "are there any more people we could add to this investment group?"

"Not likely, I'm afraid, Joe said. That's the amount Charlie will have to come up with on her own."

"Does she know this?"

"No. I haven't talked particulars with her as of yet. I figured until we knew exactly what kind of money we were looking at, there is no sense trying to conjecture."

"The way she made it seem earlier, she only had her Jeep, her stand up board and not a whole lot else. I can't imagine her coming up with $25,000."

Joe drifted off in space for a moment as if he was contemplating life. He spoke, slowly at first, almost as if he was just talking his thoughts out loud. "So….what's this business…..with her being the so-called "shark lady"?"

"I'm not sure what you're getting at."

"Well, I'm not either," Joe responded. "But it seems to me that in the last day or so, there has been some buzz around town about her being in a movie about a shark attack, or something."

"She was attacked by what I thought was a real shark when I called 911?"

"Huh? What? You called 911 about a shark attacking Charlie?"

"Yeah, it was a couple of weeks ago, but that's not important right now. But I do think that's why Ollie Farkingham put that damn mechanical shark in her bar. Something having to do with that movie. A tourist attraction I guess. Or at least that's what I thought anyway."

Just then Jamie came back to our table carrying two frosty mugs with our beer. She was ready to take our food order, but we had to apologize for having not even looked at the menu yet.

"Ya'll take your time," she said. "I'll come back to check on ya'll in a few minutes."

"Thanks, sorry about that." I said.

"No, no worries at all," Jamie responded. "Take your time!"

She then went to the table two booths down from ours. A family of five. Mother, father and three children. The two boys seemed fairly close in age, I'd guess somewhere around 10. The girl, a bit younger, maybe in the range of about 4 or so. They seemed every bit the tourists. The white sun screen still smeared on the back of each of the family's necks.

Joe and I went back to our conversation, with Joe asking "what was that movie fuss anyway?"

"Not really altogether sure. She was out paddling on her stand up board one day, the water was rough, she fell off the board and it appeared like she was being attacked by a shark. It turned out to be Ollie Farkingham's mechanical shark from the movie. Ollie was working the remote controls on it and I guess he was trying to help save her, but with it being a shark doing the saving, everyone thought she was being attacked. Guess he might have caught it on film somehow."

"She get paid for that appearance on Farkingham's film?"

"Not that I know of, but I'm not sure either."

"Hmmmm." Joe said softly to himself. "Might be something there."

"Might be something where?" I wanted to know.

"Not sure yet. But something. Let me think about this a bit and then I think we may need to visit Charlie again. Maybe even tonight."

With that Jamie swooped back down upon our table. Joe looked up, smiled and simply said, "we'll have two more beers and a couple of barbecue sandwiches. We have some thinking to do…."

Chapter Twenty-Seven. Charlie

It was finally closing time. The restaurant had been packed all day. We normally get busy, but not that busy. I flipped over the closed sign before anyone else had a chance to sneak in.

"Crazy day, huh?" Danny said as he handed me a beer.

"You're telling me."

"I know. I just told you."

I rolled my eyes and sat down at the bar for a moment. It was the first time I sat down all day. I could feel my feet aching. I wonder if those orthopedic flip-flops really work? Just the thought put a bad taste in my mouth. I banished it immediately. Lost in thought, I looked up and saw Danny had been glaring at me.

"What?" I asked.

"We ain't gonna talk about what happened here tonight?"

"We had a busy night. So what?"

"You know what I'm talkin' about," he said.

Yes, I knew what he was talking about. "Honestly, Danny, I think this whole thing is going to blow over and everyone will forget about it."

Danny shook his head. "I don't know. I surely hope not. This could be just the thing to save this here restaurant, Chuck."

"I signed a release form, not a contract. I'm not getting paid for it. My payment is that shark sitting over there."

"You ain't seen the restaurant?" He said. "I reckon if we keep up business like this, it ain't gonna matter none if you make money from the movie or not."

Danny had a point but I still think it will blow over in no time. Just then a pair of headlights shined through the window.

"We are closed," I yelled as I started shutting all the blinds. Then I caught a glimpse of a tie-dyed shirt running across the parking lot. I looked at Danny, "Is that Jamie?"

Danny looked between the blinds, "yep."

I opened the door. "What in the world are you doing here?"

"I had to come see the celebrity for myself." She hugged me. "Dude, everyone is talking about you."

"Yeah? Things were a little crazy here tonight, too."

"I had no idea you were in Ollie's new movie. I mean, I remember the whole shark attack thing but I didn't know it was for a movie."

Jamie had a tendency to ramble.

"Well, I didn't mean to be in a movie. The whole thing just kind of happened."

Danny piped in. "Been good for business too. Leastways for tonight anyway."

"Dude, that's awesome. I need your autograph or something.
Ah, man. Is that the shark? There's no way you have the shark! I totally want to ride it. Is this thing mechanical? Does its work? Have you…"

Danny quickly handed her a beer to shut her up.

"Yes," I said. "It's the shark."

There was a knock at the door.

"Is it too late to turn the lights out and hide?" I asked everyone.

Danny walked over to the door. "It's them Bob and Joe fellers," he said.

"You mean the turd wagon."

Danny gave me a look. "That turd wagon be tryin' to help you."

"I know, but he's still a turd wagon."

Jamie butted in. "Why do you need help?"

"I don't need help." I looked at Danny. "Just answer the door."
I got up from the bar to greet them. "What's up guys? Can't read signs anymore?"

They looked puzzled. "The closed sign?" I said sarcastically.

"Hey, I know you guys!" Jamie hopped up and gave them both hugs. "They were in the restaurant tonight."

I looked at Bob. "Cheater."

"How do you guys know each other?" Asked Bob.

"We're cousins!" Jamie announced. I rolled my eyes. Distant cousins.

"What brings you all here?" I asked.

There was silence for a moment, then Joe spoke up. "We wanted to talk to you about Ollie's movie."

"Who don't?" Shouted Danny from behind the bar.

"Oh my gosh, dudes. We should totally go to the movie. They're doing a special screening tonight." Jamie was way too excited.

"Don't pee yourself, Jamie." I said.

"Reckon that's not a bad idea," said Danny.

"Barf out. I would never pee my pants." Everyone ignored Jamie.

I looked over at Joe and Bob. "You guys in?"

They shook their heads yes before saying in unison, "Sure."

Once again, I reminded myself I was embracing this. If only I could turn back time. I'm afraid a nip and a tuck won't fix this.

"What the frak. Let's go."

Chapter Twenty-Eight. Bob

The Pioneer Theater on Budleigh Street in Manteo has been family owned and operated since 1918. The late H.A. Creef always said that it "wasn't a movie theater, but rather, an old timey movie house." In 1958 the theater showed former resident Andy Griffith's "No Time For Sergeants" when it was a new release. Tonight, and for the rest of this month, the theater is showing Ollie Farkingham's newest shark picture, "Nights in Nags Head." A complete rip-off of Nicholas Sparks' "Nights in Rodanthe." Rodanthe, being less than an hour drive south from the Nags Head pier, Farkingham was hoping to capitalize on the movie starring Richard Gere and Diane Lane. Ironically, during the filming of his movie, no one paid any attention to Farkingham until he, quite by accident, recorded a scene involving a shark and a local girl at the Nags Head pier. That girl, of course, the Outer Banks' newest celebrity, Charlie, "the shark girl."

We all piled into two cars. Joe, Charlie and me into my car. Jamie and Danny into Jamie's. Jamie, although having just seen it the other night, wanted to see it again. This time in the accompaniment of her now (in)famous cousin.

Before settling into our theater chairs, we all headed to the concession stand for some popcorn. The popcorn at the Pioneer Theater is almost as famous as the theater itself. Our timing was just right too, not more than five minutes later the theater went dark as the screen at the front of the house flickered to life. "Ollie Farkingham presents an Ollie Farkingham Production - Nights in Nags Head." The credits further rolled, letting us all know that not only was this a Farkinham Production, but Ollie Farkingham was the writer and the director too. A bit narcissistic if you asked me. I tried to point out to Charlie, who was sitting on my right, nestled in close, but only because the theater seats are narrow (people were thinner back in 1918), that she wasn't listed on the screen until after Ollie listed himself at least a half dozen times. But, she immediately shushed me.

The movie itself was pretty horrible. Pretty much as I had expected. The highlight of the movie was the shark "attack/rescue" of Charlie. The scene just seemed like it was edited in, but for no apparent reason. It felt like Ollie had the video, so why not just splice it into the movie?

Jamie was the first to speak as we exited the building onto Budleigh Street, heading down the block and across the street for a beer at Poor Richards. "See Cuz! You're a star! A real live star!"

Charlie, who been quiet up to now piped up, "not sure about a star. But it was pretty cool to see myself on the big screen."

As we crossed the street and went into Poor Richards, we grabbed the round table to the left of the entrance. Cindy, our server took our drink orders and then it was Joe who picked the conversation back up, "cool or not Charlie. You're in this movie and you haven't been paid for it. Unless you count having that stupid mechanical shark in your bar. And I'll even bet the only reason Ollie gave it to you was because it no longer worked and to generate publicity for his ridiculous movie. You can bet with his name plastered all over it, Ollie is making a killing on that piece of garbage film."

"Well, it's too late now, isn't it?" Charlie asked.

Now it was Danny's turn. "Chuck – it ain't never too late to take it to the man."

Yeah, Danny isn't real bright, I thought to myself. Trying to be a voice of reason I simply added "you know Charlie, you have this whole pier business to worry about. You're likely going to need some cash for that. Maybe we ought to investigate how you might get some cash from this movie."

"Why do I need cash?" Charlie asked. "Joe, didn't you say that you had investors and this whole thing could be a slam dunk."

"I did say I had a group of investors Charlie, yes." Joe said, "but I never said that they would come up with enough money to cover the entire cost of the pier. In fact, I don't think they will."

"Why didn't you tell me that earlier?"

"I didn't bring it up because I don't know what the actual numbers are going to be. We can't determine all that until the discussions with the current owners and the investors have taken place. But likely, the investors are going to want you to have some skin in the game too. That just makes good business sense."

Cindy came back to the table with our drink order. Simple enough, five Carolina Sky Blue Ales. Charlie picked hers up, stared at it for a while and took a big sip. She put it back down, and said something about needing to carry this brand at the Tiki Bar. She looked at Joe. On her face was not the expression of the confident, rebellious girl that I had come to know, but that of a scared little girl. She seemed almost fragile now.

"Joe, I don't really have anything of value to give me the skin in the game that you say is needed. I feel like everything I've worked so hard for is all of a sudden crashing to the ground."

"Don't throw in the towel just yet Charlie." Joe said trying to reassure her. "This good ol' boy might just have a trick or two still up his sleeve."

We finished up our beers in relative silence. I decided to buy the table another round before calling it a night. Charlie, Danny and Jamie loaded up into Jamie's car. Joe and I walked the block back home to Joe's house.

Tomorrow would be another day....

Chapter Twenty-Nine. Charlie

Zero part of me wanted to see the movie. I'm glad I saw it but part of me wishes I had not. I was beginning to think that Ollie Farkingham was the real turd wagon in this scenario. I was jolted back into the real world.

Jamie yelled, "Hey Chuck!" as she punched me in the arm.

"Ouch!" I punched her back.

I was not proud of what ensued. A mini cat fight that turned into hysterical laughing. Then we heard a voice from the back, "All you chicks need are wet t-shirts and I reckon this would be a dream come true."

I totally forgot Danny was in the car.

"Jamie, stop the car," I told her. "Danny, get out and walk."

"What did I do?"

"Get out."

Danny got out of the car. He walked like a dog with his tail between his legs. His house was only about 500 yards away. Danny always made an art of being dramatic.

The rest of the ride was quiet until Jamie pulled up to the restaurant. "This is you," she said.

"Not for long, I'm afraid."

"Hey, how do you know those guys?"

"Which guys?" At this point it was late and I wasn't interested in conversation.

"Joe and Bob," she said.

"They're harmless. They eat at the restaurant. Just started hanging out." I hadn't given it much thought. "I hated Joe until a few nights ago. But I was wrong about him."

"What about Bob?" she asked.

"It's a movie starring Bill Murray," I said as I shut the car door. I couldn't tell what she was getting at but I didn't like it. She was always the drama mama in the family. She wasn't starting that crap with me.

I spent most of the night googling ways to make money fast. None of them seemed very legit.

The sun started to rise. That was my cue for breakfast. Instead of a dip in the ocean, I opted for a bike ride to the Front Porch Cafe. It was Sunday. My day off. The ocean was calm. There were a few fishermen out on the pier, other than that, I was by myself. I pedaled toward the coffee shop. There is something about riding a bike that makes me feel like a kid again. Similar to the feeling I get in my stomach when going over a steep hill in a car. I took an extra lap around the parking lot to make it last a little longer.

The smell of coffee hit my nose as I opened the door. There's nothing quite like it. I ordered an egg sandwich and sat at a table. I pulled out my notebook and started jotting down ideas for songs.

"Nice to see you here, Charlie."

I looked up to see Bud, the owner of the joint.

"Hey Bud, long time no see."

"It's an honor to have the town celebrity in our midst."

I punched him in the arm.

"Let me check on your sandwich," he said as he pretended to rub his wounded arm.

He came back and set the sandwich down in front of me. "Be careful, the plate is hot."

I gave him a "no shit" look.

"Are you entering in the contest?" he asked.

"What contest? And probably not."

"Ragamuffin Ukuleles is putting on a contest. The winner gets a sponsorship deal worth $20,000 and headlines a weekend at the Savannah Theatre in Georgia."

I'm normally not a contest person but this seemed intriguing. He handed me the flyer hanging on his wall. "You'd be perfect for it."

I stared at the flyer almost in disbelief. "Thanks, Bud."

"Enjoy your breakfast, Chuck."

I folded the flyer and put it in my notebook. This could help save the restaurant. I had to do it.

Chapter Thirty. Bob

Bruno, my cat, and I took a paddle this morning in the sound. The water was calm and inviting as I hoisted Bruno onto the front of my board. The stares I get from people when they see my cat on the nose of my paddle board never ceases to amaze me. Maybe I should start a web series and call it "Bruno – The World Champion Paddling Cat." The thought made me chuckle.

Following our paddle Bruno was looking a little raggedy, so I figured now might be a good time to get him groomed over at "Tail Waggers" in the Sea Gate North Shopping Center in Kill Devil Hills. Maybe stop at Barefoot Bernies for a crab cake sandwich for lunch while waiting for Bruno to be finished.

I got in my car and started the half-hour drive to Kill Devil Hills. The air was salty. The sun was high in the sky. As I crossed the Washington Baum Bridge on the Manteo - Nags Head Causeway, boats were departing from Pirate's Cove Marina out for a day on the water. Either they were locals playing hooky from work, or vacationers enjoying their stay on these barrier islands. I couldn't be sure from my vantage point at the crest of the bridge. Traffic was moderately heavy; pretty much like you would expect during tourist season, but I made it to the groomer relatively easy.

Amber, the groomer, who had answered the phone when I called ahead, greeted me at the counter. She was blonde, with short hair, very tanned and had a primitive looking surfer tattoo on her right shoulder that poked out of her white tank top. Very pleasant girl who had said that she had lived here all her life. She didn't know anything other than the Outer Banks. She took to Bruno immediately.

"What breed of cat is Bruno?" Amber asked.

"What I've been told by my vet, he's a Norwegian Forest Cat." I added

"My, look at that bushy tail."

"Looks just like a raccoon," I said proudly.

"Bruno is a beautiful cat" Amber said. With all this fur, you might want to give me a good hour or so. There is a lot of fur to be groomed, that's for sure."

"Sounds good. I'm just gonna run down the street to Barefoot Bernie's and grab a sandwich."

"Cool but make sure you tell them you're waiting on your cat here and they'll give you 10% discount."

"Awesome. Thanks!"

I made the couple of minute trip to Barefoot Bernies and had a seat at the bar. Figured I'd leave the tables open for the soon to be arriving lunch crowd. No sooner than placing my order for a Red Stripe and crab cake sandwich did I get a huge whack on my back.

Stunned, I turned around quickly, "Danny! Would you PLEASE stop doing that!"

"Sorry boss." Danny replied.

"Why aren't you out at the Tiki Bar working? Why are you here?" I said in my most annoyed sounding voice.

"I don't start work for 'nother hour. And I AM allowed to go to other places too you know."

"Yeah Danny, I guess you are at that. Where's your wife? Why doesn't she ever come out with you?"

"She don't never want to leave the yard. She and that damn dog of hers. All he does is bark. They go out back and do some fishin' in the sound. The whole time, that fool dog barkin' too. She don't like people too much I expect. Not the wife. Not the dog neither."

"Ah, gotcha. Sounds like a good marriage you got there."

"Well, it is what it is" Danny answered. "So sausage guy, let me ask you, you reckon Charlie's gonna be able to save our jobs on the pier? Or should I start lookin' for something else?"

"I don't know the answer to that right now Danny. What I do know is that my cousin Joe is out meeting with the owners right now to set up some sort of meeting with them and the investors. I guess we'll know soon enough."

Just then my food was brought out and sat down in front of me. Crab cake sandwich and fries. And it was fabulous too. Danny sat there and just watched. I offered half of my crab cake sandwich and fries to him, which he took almost too enthusiastically. Made me a bit sad. Things are probably tight for him. Didn't sound like his wife worked all that much so he's likely to be the sole bread winner at the house. And he couldn't make all that much money working as the handy man down at the Tiki Bar.

As I was finishing "half" my lunch, my cell phone rang. I figured it was Amber at Tail Waggers letting me know that Bruno was ready; but the caller ID showed it to be Cousin Joe.

As I started to answer it, Danny said quickly, "I gotta run to work, thanks for the lunch."

"You bet Danny." I then turned my attention to the ringing phone. "Hey Joe what's up?"

"Where's Charlie? I just set up a meeting.".....

Chapter Thirty-One. Charlie

I woke up in time to catch the sunrise. With my coffee in hand, it seemed like a perfect morning. I grabbed my camera and snapped a few pictures. I checked my phone and realized the battery died. I went inside to the studio, plugged my phone in, and started to work on a few new coffee mugs.

I heard the back door open, it must be Danny. He turned the corner and looked disheveled as ever. His hair looked like it had not been combed. His clothes were wrinkled and half thrown on. "Look what the cat drug in," I said trying to lighten the mood.

He would have given me a dirty look had it not been for the 15 years worth of baggage showing up under his eyes this morning. He threw up a hand to acknowledge me and went in the kitchen. He was more quiet than usual. I followed him.

"Are you okay, Danny?"

He half mumbled something but I wasn't sure I wanted him to repeat it. I started making a new batch of coffee and some eggs and toast. He sat down and put his head in his hands. I was going to say something but decided silence was more appropriate. I finished the eggs and poured his coffee. He gobbled it up and cleaned his dishes after. I went back to the studio to finish the mugs I started earlier.

I overheard Danny talking on the phone. I couldn't make out who he was talking to but I could tell he was trying to talk low. When he finished he came into the studio. "Hey," he said. "I'm gonna run outside right quick. I won't be long."

Before I could answer he was out the door.

I went into the dining room and prepared the tables for opening. I looked out the window and saw Jamie out by the pier. I was going to step outside to say hello but then I saw Danny. They seemed to be in an argument. I couldn't tell what was going on but this definitely didn't seem like a "you owe me five bucks" kind of talk. They seemed amicable at the end. They hugged. I went back to setting out the salt, pepper, and hot sauce in an effort to disguise my snooping.

Danny walked back in. I so badly wanted to ask what the hell he was doing. Instead I said, "What's up?"

He gave me a cool head nod.

Danny was definitely being weird. And I had no idea what was going on between those two. Honestly, I didn't care. I had a restaurant to save. I went back to the studio and signed up for the ukulele competition. At this point, I will take my chances with anything. It's at least worth a shot.

I flipped over the "open" sign. People were lined up outside, waiting. I hadn't even noticed. Ollie Farkingham walked through the door. With reporters. He was being interviewed. A mob of people followed him.

"Are you kidding me?" I said, but no one heard me. I walked over to Ollie. "What's this all about?"

"And here she is!" He put his arm around my shoulders like we were best buds. "The star of the movie!" Camera flashes started going off like we were at the Olympics and I just performed a triple axel. I was a bit stunned. I stood there not knowing what to say. Ollie couldn't have been more self-indulgent. He led everyone to the shark. "Here's the co-star of the movie!" The bulbs started flashing again.

I looked around the restaurant; everyone was watching the circus taking place.

I finally got my wits about me and walked over to Ollie. Before I got there a reporter stepped in front of me and shoved a microphone in my face. "What do you think of Ollie's masterpiece being nominated for an Emmy in the short film category?"

"An Emmy? That piece of crap?"

"Yes!" She shoved the microphone back in my face.

"I have a restaurant to run." I walked over to Ollie. "You have five minutes to get this freak show out of here."

A reporter shoved his card in my hand as I walked away. "Call me. Let's chat," he said.

I took the card in hopes it would shut him up and walked back to the studio for some quiet. I forgot my phone was still on the charger. I had missed a call from Joe. I had a text that read: Got a meeting set up. Call me as soon as you can.

Chapter Thirty-Two. Joe

I'm not sure what I just saw on the local news access channel right now, but apparently there was some sort of zoo happening down at Chuck's Grub & Tiki Bar. The sound was muted in the meeting room so I couldn't hear anything, but the picture showed the mechanical shark, Ollie and Charlie. Oh well, can't think about that right now. I've got a meeting to prep for.

My thoughts were soon interrupted by Kyle, the server from the Kill Devil Hills Comfort Inn. He had come into the room to start setting out the continental breakfast I had ordered for today's meeting. Nothing elaborate; coffee, orange juice, assortment of danish, bagels and some cut-up fruit. Not knowing this ahead of time, but apparently at night, this meeting room doubles up as the Outer Banks Comedy Club. Their stage and backdrop still set up on the wall off to the right of our conference table.

Not more than five minutes after Kyle finished up his duties, the meeting participants started to arrive. First to walk in were the pier owners, followed by five potential investors. And nearly everyone was already on their second cup of coffee when Charlie finally decided to show up. If first impressions are important, well she didn't make a good one.

I opened the meeting by welcoming the group. I was glad to see that cousin Bob hadn't come. This really wasn't his affair after all. I stated the purpose of the meeting, which was to see if there was any interest at all from the current owners of the pier to open a second set of negotiations for the sale of the Nags Head Pier.

Mike, the pier's owner was the first to speak. "Lady and gentlemen, as you know, my wife and I are in the process of selling the Nags Head Fishing Pier. We have already started speaking to Dare County, so I really don't know what we can or will accomplish here. The only reason I agreed to this get together was because neither my wife nor I wish to see Charlie out on the street. The county has plans for that space that would entail the restaurant being closed."

With my eyes firmly on Charlie, hoping that she would respond to Mike's opening remarks, I decided to interject. "Thanks Mike. Full disclosure here. While technically an employee of Dare County, I am not here on their behalf. In fact, that is not even the part of the county I work for."

"Yeah, there's no dogs on the loose here," George, one of the investors chimed in, as the rest of the crowd let out a nervous laugh.

"As I was saying, I am here as more of a liaison for Mike and Randi, the current owners of the pier. They know, and I know, that the county does not move very fast. They really would prefer to sell this asset before the year is out and that is not likely to happen with the county."

"Let's be clear too," Randi said. "Yes, we would like to sell the pier this year, but I know speaking for my husband too, that is not our main goal in speaking with ya'll. We are here because we like Charlie and her restaurant. We want to be fair."

George, one of the largest property owners on the Outer Banks, decided to cut right to the chase. "Mike and Randi, we've known each other for a long time."

"About 35 years I'd say," added Mike.

"Yeah, likely it has been that long" George continued. Just what kind of price are you looking to get out of your pier?"

"What do you think its worth George?" Mike replied.

"Oh no. Don't throw that back on me. You know I bought land on the Outer Banks for 50 cents an acre back in the 1950's. Well before this was the tourist area that it is now. I won't play that game with you. You tell us all the price for that rickety wooden pier of yours."

Mike chuckled when he heard George refer to his pier as "rickety." Although it appeared to have made Randi mad, as she immediately furrowed her brow upon hearing that word. "Well George, you always have been a crusty ol' codger. Not one for pleasantries and certainly not one for handing out compliments."

George smiled to himself. This has always been the way he conducted his business. He worked very hard at cultivating that image.

"So we'll cut right to the chase as you like to say. I won't tell you what our negotiations with the county have stated. Because frankly, we haven't even gotten to that point yet. But if you fine folks can pony up $5 million, I'd say we have an agreement for me to terminate my talks with the county."

"Five million dollars for THAT RICKETY old pier?" George shouted out. The other four investors and Charlie seeming content to let Mike and George duke this thing out.

"Why, that pier isn't worth half that!" Said George, spitting out his words.

"Maybe not to you." Mike said.

"Not to anyone!" George interjected.

It was time for me to calm things down and soothe some feelings, so I jumped in. "Boys, boys, boys. We can work this out in a civil manner." As I started to continue, George got up and got himself another cup of coffee and a danish.

"If I'm gonna be robbed like this, I might as well load up on the free food," George said.

I continued, "George this is just a preliminary meeting. Just to gauge if there is any interest in moving forward with this group."

"Well, Joe, George and everyone else," Mike said, "Randi and I came here because we were asked to. If the $5 million is too rich for your blood, then we understand. Really we do. But that's the price we've set for it. We will just continue our talks with the county instead. I think at this point my wife and I will leave now. Charlie, gentlemen, have a good day."

With that, Mike led his wife Randi out of the meeting room.

George, as gruff as everyone expected him to be, climbed the Comedy Club stage ready to pontificate to the remainder of the meeting participants. "Ya'll can be taken for a ride if you want. But I've been buying property on this sand pile for longer than most of you have been alive. Hell, I've rented and sold property and houses to most of your mama's and daddy's. This offer is a sham, and I'll advise you to not take part." With that, George stepped down from the stage and exited the room.

In hopes of keeping this deal alive, I turned to the remaining four potential investors and Charlie and asked for their thoughts.

Kirk, a young budding entrepreneur who at 29 had already made his first million dollars several times over in the restaurant business was the first to respond. "Wouldn't surprise me if George didn't want this deal to himself. Probably why he huffed and he puffed and tried to dissuade us from pursuing this thing."

"I agree with Kirk." I responded. "I think George is just trying to throw everyone else off the trail. But do you think the rest of you can put this deal together without him, or even want to?"

Kirk responded again, "Charlie, for me anyway, I would need to know that if we bought this thing that you would continue to rent that space and agree to keep the restaurant going."

Charlie, who had felt she was in way over her head at this meeting, and who hadn't said a word since arriving, managed to get out, "well, of course it would depend on what the rent was. If it was in the same ballpark as it is now, then yes. I would love to stay."

"Ok boys," Kirk said to the rest of the group. I'm still in and I would prefer to do this thing without George. All those in favor, please raise your hands."

Immediately, the other four investors hands shot upwards, toward the ceiling.

Chapter Thirty-Three. Chuck's Tiki Bar

Closed for the day

Chapter Thirty-Four. Joe

"Joe this had better be good!" Charlie screamed as she came barreling through the front door of my house. No knock, no nothing. She just came flying through the front door, with her maintenance guy Danny in tow, who was trying to look tough, but not quite pulling it off.

"Whoa, Charlie slow down. What's the problem?" Cousin Bob asked.

"What's the problem? WHAT'S THE PROBLEM?!?!?!" Your lame brained cousin, county worker Joe here, called and said I had to meet him immediately. I tried explaining that I had a business to run, but he couldn't wait. I've NEVER had to close the Tiki Bar before. I mean, you know for a hurricane, but not for no reason!"

Now, all eyes turned to me. "Yes, Charlie, it is imperative that I had you come over now, that's true. But think of it this way, you can close the bar for one day, or you can close it for good. It's really your choice."

"Well I made my choice and I'm here Joe. What is so gosh fired important?"

"Wait, not yet. We have to wait for one other person before we start." I said.

"Start what?" Danny wanted to know.

Keeping in mind that Danny isn't the "sharpest tool in the shed" and not really understanding why he was there to begin with, I decided to be tactful. "I want to move forward our initial meeting from the other day. And I needed you here to do it. Out of the public eye as they say. We have one more person arriving. In fact his text indicated that he'd be here in less than five minutes. While we're waiting may I offer you and Danny a drink?"

Danny, not surprisingly jumped in first and said he'd love a beer. Charlie said to make it two.

"Excellent. Bob, would you do me a favor and get all of us a beer while we wait."

"Be happy to" Bob said. Charlie could've sworn she heard him add under his breath, "What am I? Your damn slave?" That made her chuckle to herself.

Bob got up from the pleather winged back chair he was sitting in and went into the kitchen to retrieve four cold Coronas. He smiled as he handed Charlie hers. She smiled back. Bob took notice of that and sat back down in his chair.

Once each person swallowed their first sip, I heard the tires of the Chevy Suburban belonging to our next guest, crunch on the gravel below my house in the driveway. Before he was able make it to the top of the steps leading into the house, Danny announced he was ready for a second beer. Although annoyed I told him to go help himself, but reminded him that this is a serious business meeting and not a fraternity party.

As Danny reached into the refrigerator for his beer, the last remaining meeting participant came cheerily through the door and in a sing-song voice said "Good afternoon all. It's a fabulous day on the Outer Banks!"

Dressed in perfectly creased khakis, a pink golf shirt and boat shoes, it was Kirk Bashnagel, the multi-millionaire restaurateur. Kirk was the one who spearheaded the drive to cut George out in the last meeting. It appears as though he cut out more than just George since none of the other investors are now part of this meeting.

"Charlie, sorry for the last minute notice on this," Kirk began. "I wanted to have this meeting quickly, before anyone else had the same idea. And I apologize for the cloak and dagger part of it too, but well, better we're not all seen together."

"Well, I had to close my restaurant today to be here. I'm quite sure you didn't have to suffer the same loss of business in your properties," Charlie said with a bit of annoyance in her voice. "Just what do you have in mind Mr Bashnagel?"

"Please Charlie. Its Kirk. If we're going to be partners, we don't need to stand on formalities."

"Ok Kirk" spat out Danny, trying to be important in the meeting. We're here. Charlie and me. What do you want that it has to be top secret?"

Kirk looked at Charlie, who with a nod of the head indicated that it was ok to speak in front of Danny. "Charlie, I had a conversation with Mike and Randi following our initial meeting. I agreed in principle with them to purchase the pier. We're still in negotiations over the final price, but it will be close enough to their asking price that they've decided to back out of the talks with the county. We've also agreed to not include George in the deal. I just can't work with that man. Too vulgar and condescending for my tastes. And I see no reason to include the others either. Too many chefs as they say…"

"Yeah, I heard people say that before" Danny interjected. "Never knew quite what it meant, but I heard people say it."

Before continuing Kirk looked over to me and said the beer looked refreshing and asked if he might have one. As I got him one, he continued.

"Here's the deal. I've asked you here to be my partner. I've included Joe because he brought us all together. I only thought it right that he should get some sort of fee for brokering our deal. Now, his cousin Bob, well I don't know him, but he's asked to join us in the deal. Said he's thinking of relocating here and is looking for an investment."

I noticed the quick shift of Charlie's attention from Kirk over to my cousin and the smile both gave each other.

"Of course," Kirk continued. "I told him that was totally your call. If you wanted to share your piece, that would be up to you."

Charlie, who had now calmed down since she came crashing through the front door a half-hour ago, said "Of course. I would welcome Bob in the deal. But I guess we should talk about this "deal." If you're proposing us to be equal partners I have to tell you, I cannot come up with two and a half million dollars!"

"I'm sorry Charlie. Perhaps you misunderstood. I'm not proposing that we be equal partners at all. In fact, I wouldn't do this deal if I had to split it with others. That's why I splintered from the group to do it on my own. My proposal for you is that I would own the pier, but that you would continue to lease the space. I've seen your current contract with Mike and Randi and I'm comfortable with the numbers."

"Well, if that's all it is, then I'm not sure we had to have this big top-secret meeting then. Basically nothing changes for me. I'll just be your tenant instead of Mike and Randi's."

"Not quite Charlie. I don't do business that way. I'm not looking strictly for a tenant. I can get that anywhere. See, I don't want to have to worry about the pier. I want to know that once the deal is done I don't have to think about it anymore so I can move onto my next investment. So what I want is for you to be a minority owner. And I mean, a big minority owner. But enough of an owner that I have the security knowing you won't just up and leave once your lease is up. I want to know that it would also be in your best interest to stay."

"Makes sense to me," I said.

"Me too" said Danny. Not like anyone cared if it made sense at all to Danny.

Charlie thought about it briefly before saying anything. When she did, she moved over to where my cousin Bob was sitting. "Exactly what do you need out of me Mr Bashna……Kirk?"

"Charlie, I think if you came up with $50,000, that would be enough in the pot for me to be secure that you would stick around. Now, with Joe's cousin here wanting to be part of the deal, I'll leave it up to you two to decide who contributes what."

"Fifty-thousand! That means much more to me than it does to you," Charlie said.

"Yes, I'm sure it does Charlie" replied Kirk. But I think its a fair number."

Charlie looked down to my cousin Bob, "What do you think sausage guy?"

"I think $50,000 is a lot of money Charlie, but if you're willing to go for it, then so am I."

I thought how strange that my cousin, who didn't even know this girl two weeks ago was willing to turn his back on everything in Ohio and go into a business costing him potentially tens of thousands of dollars. Money that I'm not even sure he has. But there he was in my living room doing just that.

"Kirk" said Charlie extending a hand. "I'm not sure yet how I will come up with $50,000, but you have a deal."

While everyone else was high fiving and shaking hands, Danny went back to the refrigerator and helped himself to a third beer…..

Chapter Thirty-Five. Charlie

The ride home was quiet except for the texting Danny was doing on his phone. He had a weird smile on his face. I turned onto his street, he looked up when we got to his driveway, "Keep driving. Keep driving!"

Confused, I slowed down. "What?"

"Keep driving. I'm not going home."

"Okay…where am I taking you?"

"Lucky 12."

I turned around, still a little confused. "Why are you going to Lucky 12, Danny?"

He got a blank look on his face. I could tell he was thinking hard. "Because Chuck's is closed. Yeah. Chuck's is closed."

"Danny, do me a favor. Don't ever get in trouble with the police."

He looked puzzled. I would say that's his normal face but this looked more puzzled than usual.

"Why?"

"Because you're a lousy liar."

Danny ignored the comment and went back to his phone. The rest of the ride was quiet. I pulled up to Lucky 12 and let him out.

"Be careful, Danny."

He shut the door and walked away, unsure that he even heard me. I had no idea what was going on there but I had no time to worry about it. I had bigger fish to fry.

It was weird pulling into the empty parking lot of the restaurant. It would normally be hopping. Unsure of what to do next, I decided to text Bob.

Chuck: Hey

I saw the bubbles pop up. He was writing something.

Bob: Hey

What do I say next? No more bubbles.

Chuck: Thanks for having my back earlier today. You have no idea how much that means.

Bob: I always have your back.

H-m-m. I wanted to ask him over. I wanted to see him. Away from everybody and away from everything. Part of me was afraid. What if he says no? I'm being ridiculous.

Chuck: Want to come over? I sent it as is. I hurried up and followed it up with…
Chuck: You know, to talk about everything.

I waited for the bubbles. No bubbles. Maybe he set his phone down. Maybe he had to go do something real quick. Maybe…

BUBBLES!

Bob: Sure. Sounds good to me.

Woohoo!

Chuck: Maybe bring your SUP gear.

Bob: Ok. I will be on my way.

Chuck: Okay.

Okay? Okay. This is good. I went upstairs and found myself changing clothes and "freshening up" a bit. Wait, what am I doing? I looked out the window to see Bob's car pull in the parking lot. I felt a little nervous going to the door. I didn't know why. He walked up to the door. He looked unsure of whether to knock or just open the door. I waved and did the honors.

"Hey, Bob." I found myself hugging him.

He seemed a little caught off-guard. "Hey, Charlie."

We both stood looking at each other. An awkward moment passed before I spoke. "I'm glad you could come."

"Me too."

"Did you bring your paddleboard stuff?"

"It's in the car."

"We could have our meeting out on the water?"

"Sure," he said.

I went upstairs to change and told Bob to use the bathroom downstairs. We met back on the beach. I caught Bob looking at me. Usually I would make a smart ass comment but today I didn't seem to mind. We grabbed our boards and paddled out. Instead of standing, we mainly sat and talked. The water was calm. We watched the sunset to the west.

"I don't know how I'm going to come up with the money, Bob,"

Bob sat silently for a little bit. "We will figure it out."

"We better be doing some figuring real fast."

"Your business has increased since the movie, right?"

I shook my head "yes." But not $50,000 better."

"But it's something." I could tell he was trying to reassure me.

"I also signed up for a ukulele competition. The winner gets $20,000."

Bob smiled. "See, it will all work out." He paused for moment as if just remembering something. "You also have the movie. Ollie owes you some money."

"I don't know. It's worth a try I guess." My faith in Ollie was about as good as telling someone to buy a house and not get hurricane insurance. "I should start a "Save Chuck's" campaign. I could do mugs, maybe a song. We could get the shark fixed so it doesn't hurt people."

We both laughed at the thought of the shark.

"But I'm serious. We should make this a real grassroots effort."

Bob nodded in agreement.

"I have the number for the reporter that wanted to interview me. This would be great exposure."

"That's a great idea, Charlie. You should definitely do that."

It was nice having someone other than Danny to talk to. Bob and I paddled into shore. We took turns in the outdoor shower. We went inside and grabbed a couple of beers. We sat at the bar, closer to each other than usual.

"I'm glad you came here."

"Of course. I'm always here to help."

"No, I mean, I'm glad you came here that first night. I'm happy to know you."

We both leaned in a little closer. Then Danny came busting through the door.

"Hey, dudes!"

Danny stumbled to the bar to grab another beer. Bob got up from his stool. "I think you have had enough, Danny. It's time to go home."

Danny was unsure what to think. He didn't have many thoughts to begin with, add beer and it gets worse. "What're you guys doing?"

"Danny, go home." I hated seeing him like this.

Bob looked at me and said "I got this. Don't worry."

He grabbed Danny's arm and started dragging him outside. I reached for Bob's hand. We clasped for a moment. "Thank you," I whispered.

Chapter Thirty-Six. Bob

I grabbed Danny's arm and started dragging him outside. As I did, Charlie reached for my hand and whispered, "Thank you." I still don't know what is going on there. She invited me over. She "said" to have a meeting, but it felt different than just a regular "business meeting." It felt like that was just an excuse to get me over. I don't know, I'm just really bad at reading signals from the opposite sex. It's usually just me reading more into innocent exchanges than there really is….

But for the here and now, I have to do something with this inebriated handyman. I threw him into my car and buckled him in. "Danny, you're a bad drunk," I said.

"And you're a good friend, not the sausage guy," Danny slurred back. "I still don't know what that means. What that mean, Bob?"

"Nothing, Danny. Don't worry about it. Where did you just come from?"

"I was talking to Jamie over at the Lucky 12. I think she's sweet on me. Kissed me on the jaw once."

"Charlie's cousin Jamie? The one that went to the movie with us?"

"Jamie's my sweetheart" Danny said, holding back what I thought was going to be vomit all over my front seat. I opened the passenger side window and suggested that he stick his head out while we're driving to Wanchese.

"You want me to sit here like my wife's damn fool dog does in the car? Head out the window and tongue hanging out of my mouth?"

"Well, Danny, if it keeps you from throwing up in my car, then yes."

Just then we passed the Lucky 12 as we made our way down the Beach Road towards Wanchese and Danny's house.

"Wait! Wait! Take me there Bob! I wanna go see Jamie!"

"Danny, what about your wife?"

"Oh, she don't care. She don't never leave the house and she don't care nuthin' 'bout what I do. Take me back to the Lucky 12!"

Reluctantly, I turned the car around in the parking lot of the souvenir shop T-shirt Whirl, heading back to Lucky 12. I figured I'd go in for a beer and see if there is anything to this Jamie - Danny thing.

"Ok Danny. But I'm only going in for one beer. Then I'm out and I'm taking you home."

"Ok Bob" Danny said, continuing to slur. I only need a few minutes to mesmerize sweet Jam, that's what I call her, Jam, my lil' nickname for her. I'll bust out some sweet dance moves and she'll be impressed with this handyman. Or as I like to say, handyDUDE."

"Ok Danny, whatever you say."

We pulled into the lot and immediately we were met by a guy who can only be described as being twice the size of an NFL lineman. All six foot six, 250 pounds of him came charging at my car yelling that he was going to kill us. Just then Danny yelled out "Back in the car and get out of here! Go! Go! Go!"

As I put the car back into drive and squealed the tires peeling out onto the Beach Road, I finally mustered enough strength to spit out at Danny "What the hell was that?"

"Oh that weren't nothin'. That was Jam's boyfriend."

"Boyfriend?!?!?! What do you mean boyfriend? You said she was sweet on you. Kissed you on the jaw you said."

"She did! Back when we were in high school."

"High School?!?!?! Danny what are you, like 30 by now?"

"I'm only 29 Bob!"

"Well, I think you outlived your welcome at yet another place here on the Outer Banks. I'm taking you back home. I'm way too busy to be babysitting you."

We rode back to Wanchese in silence. I pulled into Danny's yard and immediately heard the dog bark. I then heard Danny mutter under his breath some sort of expletive as he struggled to open the passenger door on my car. He got out, staggered a bit, fell twice trying to climb the four steps to the house and finally grabbed the handle on the screen door, after reaching for it twice and missing it. He finally fell through the front door when I heard his wife berate him. Much like she did the first time I was here to drop him off. I couldn't help feel a bit sorry for him as I put the Jeep into drive and started back for my cousin's house on Eleanor Dare Place in Manteo.

Chapter Thirty-Seven. ABC 11

Good morning. This is Duffy Dixon reporting live from Chuck's Grub & Tiki Bar on the Nag's Head pier. It was not long ago that I stood here in this very spot reporting the near drowning and then miraculous save of the owner Charlie Foster. Since then she has become somewhat of a celebrity with a cameo in Ollie Farkingham's new movie. But it hasn't been all ups for Charlie. She recently found out that the owners of the pier are selling out and in turn selling her out. Charlie, in your own words, tell us the situation you currently find yourself in.

Thanks, Duffy. I will try to use my own words; I'm not sure who else's I would use. Anyway, many of you watching know me as Chuck from the Tiki Bar. It's all I have ever known. It's my whole life. It seems that when it comes to money and business, people don't care how their decisions affect others. I know Chuck's is classified somewhat as a bar, but I have always run my business thinking of the families that this business supports. With that said, I have to raise $50,000.00 in very short time in order to keep Chuck's from going out of business.

Sorry for interrupting Charlie, but are you saying that Chuck's will be forced to close if you don't come up with the required money?

That's correct, Duffy. This brings me to my next point: we are a tight knit community and I would like to think that we come together to help each other out. I am starting a SAVE CHUCK'S campaign at the Tiki Bar. I will be selling handmade shirts and mugs and I will even customize them for the customers. There will also be mechanical shark rides - the same shark that "saved" me, and a donation box. In addition to that I will be competing in the ukulele competition with a $20,000.00 cash prize. I could use all the support we can get.

Mechanical shark rides? That sounds exciting! You heard it here first, folks. The SAVE CHUCK's campaign is alive and running. Come out and support one of our favorite hometown gals and keep one of our favorite restaurants alive and running. Anything else you want to add, Charlie?

Save Chuck's!

All right, folks. Remember you heard it here first. Come out and support Chuck's Grub & Tiki Bar. Listen to some music, snag a mug or shirt, you can even take a spin on the infamous shark that saved our girl Charlie and is featured in the movie.

Reporting live from Chuck's Grub & Tiki Bar at the Nag's Head pier, this is Duffy Dixon, ABC 11.

Chapter Thirty-Eight. Bob

"Wow! Your girl is getting some airplay from Channel 11." Cousin Joe said to me.

"Yeah, reckon she is."

"Reckon? RECKON?!?!? You're down here less than two weeks and you're now using "reckon" as an everyday word?"

Sheepishly, I looked at my cousin, who by the way, is pretty much the antithesis of any of the real locals I've yet to run across. I mean, who in the middle of summer wears a full suit to work everyday anyway? Especially when you don't have to? Slowly I answered him. "Yup. Reckon I do now."

Cousin Joe just shook his head and walked out of the room. As he did I called out to him. "Hey I'm going to run over to the beach to see Charlie. See if she needs some help on this Save Chuck's campaign. You want to go?"

Joe stopped and slowly turned back to me. "I'll tell you the truth cousin Bob," almost spitting the last two words out rather than just saying them. "I kinda wish that maybe Charlie took a different tact here. That interview really made it seem like Mike and Randi, the pier owners, were some sort of villains. Threatening to throw Charlie out if she didn't cough up 50 G's." Joe continued as I noticed the vein in his neck start to stick out as he spoke. "You do remember of course, it was Mike and Randi who tracked me down to see if a deal could be put together so Charlie didn't have to leave. Now she's making it appear that they are the big, bad landlord about to throw this sweet innocent little girl out in the street on her keister. I'll tell you what cuz, if it were me, I might think about pulling this deal off the table and just go back to dealing with the county." Joe paused, no doubt for effect before continuing. "I just hope for her sake, for your sake, and for Kirk's sake, that they just don't go ahead and do that."

I was startled by Joe's reaction to Charlie's interview. But I also knew that he was personal friends with Mike and Randi. So he might have some insight as to how they think. I, of course, was hoping he was wrong. I started down the stairs toward my car but then I quickly turned around and went back into the house. "Joe, you really think they may take it that way?"

As if to mock me, Joe answered, "yeah, I reckon they might."

"You think maybe we should take some precautionary measure here and contact them to let them know that wasn't the way Charlie intended that interview to go?"

"Honestly. That's not for you or I to do. I don't think it would mean a thing coming from us. I think that is something Charlie needs to do. She created this potential mess. She needs to be the one to clean it up. Wouldn't hurt for her to place a call to Kirk either to apologize to him for maybe screwing his deal up."

"Anything else?" I wanted to know.

"Yeah. One of you should probably contact Duffy over at the TV station. See if you could get a follow up interview scheduled so she can clarify this thing."

"Gotcha. OK, thanks. I'm going to head down to the pier to get some of this damage control started."

As I walked out of the house back down towards my car I heard Joe mutter behind me, "yeah good luck with all that…"

I got into my Jeep, and started driving towards the beach. It would take about 15 minutes to get to the pier so I decided to start with the TV station. I dialed up their number….

On the second ring a perky young women drawled into the phone with a sultry southern accent, "Hello Channel 11, Your Outer Banks ABC News and Weather Home, this is Bonnie, how may I assist you?"

"Hi Bonnie" I replied. "I'm looking for Duffy Dixon. He around?"

"I'm sorry sir. He isn't. He just finished up a live interview and he and the crew are packing up their gear and heading back. But I can connect you with his cell phone if you'd like,"

"Yes Bonnie, please. That would be wonderful."

"Thanks. Ya'll have a great day sir."

With that, Bonnie transferred me over to Duffy's cell. The person that answered didn't sound nearly as nice as the person I just watched on the air with Charlie. "Yeah, this is Dixon. What do you need?"

"Uh. Hi Mr Dixon."

"Don't need no Mister" the voice on the other end said. "Just state your business. I'm very busy at the moment."

"Yes, of course. Sorry." I continued, trying to sound as authoritative as I could muster. "My name is Bob Evans…"

"The sausage guy?"

"No Mr Dixon….errr, Duffy, not the sausage guy. We just have the same name."

"Weird. Well, what do you want Evans? Like I said, I've got things to do."

"Yes, this will only take a second. I represent the Save Chuck's Campaign. I was hoping we could schedule a follow up interview with you. You know, kind of a here's where we are now kind of a thing."

"No, thanks. We got what we needed out of that first interview. Don't think we need to worry about a follow up."

"But don't you think Mr...., I mean Duffy, that people would like to keep up with how it's all working out?"

"Look Evans. My TV station doesn't exist to be a arm of the Charlie Foster marketing team. Right now I don't see a need for a follow up. If the people want to know how your campaign is doing, they'll either stop down for a beer or for dinner to check in on it. Or they can read it in the newspaper. Me? I got a lot of other stories I can run with."

"But...."

"But nothing Evans. I got to go."

With that the phone clicked off. I then tried to gather my thoughts for the last three or four minutes of my drive to the Nags Head Pier. My first objective didn't go well. I was hoping the second one will.

As I pulled into the parking lot of the pier, Charlie came running out to greet me. "Did you see my interview with Duffy? Charlie asked.

"I did." I replied. "And we have to talk."

Ten minutes later I returned to the parking lot and my Jeep. I did not expect that to have happened…..

Chapter Thirty-Nine. Charlie

What a night. I could not have asked for the interview with Duffy to go any better than it did. I finally feel like there is some hope in this whole mess. I knew it was getting late and there was a lot of work to do, but I couldn't get my mind off Bob. I needed to share this with him. I picked up the phone and began dialing his number when I saw his car pull into the parking lot. I felt my heart jump; a bolt of excitement ran through my body. He must have seen the interview. I should have known he was watching. Before he could get out of his car, I ran to the parking lot to meet him. "Did you see my interview with Duffy?"

He slowly stepped toward me. "I did." He stared at his flip-flops and reluctantly looked up at me. "We have to talk"

"Are you okay?" I asked.

"Can we go inside?"

"Sure." I said.

Our walk into the restaurant was long. The sound of his dumb flip-flops overtaking most of the silence. I still didn't understand orthopedic flip-flops. I walked up to the bar. "Want a beer?"

He nodded his head. "Sure."

I grabbed a Kitty Hawk Blonde and handed it to him. "So what's up? Why so serious? I thought this would have been more of a celebration."

"Joe and I saw the interview. You did so well. I was so proud of you."

"Okay, so what's the problem?" I asked.

"Joe thinks you could lose the place because of that interview."

"Wait. What?"

"He thinks you made Mike and Randi look like villains. He's afraid they might pull the plug on the whole deal."

I could feel my blood boiling. "Are you kidding me? I made them look like villains? How about the fact that they want to take my restaurant away from me? The restaurant my dad ran and I took over. Am I supposed to quit and let it all go? I don't think so. I'm not going down without a fight."

I slammed my beer down on the table. The bottle broke and beer was running everywhere. "I'll grab some towels," said Bob.

"I will get the broom. Watch the broken –"

Bob screamed as I heard a huge thud. I was almost afraid to look. "Are you okay?"

"I reckon I just lost my footing." He said.

"Did you just say reckon?"

Bob nodded. I shook my head.

Then Bob said, "Can't a guy say reckon?"

"Don't change the subject." I said. "I'm not giving up this restaurant."

"Joe just thinks you might need to tone it down a little. Maybe apologize to Mike and Randi."

"Apologize?" I slammed my fist down on the table, hitting all of the broken glass. Pain shot through my wrist. Blood was dripping down my arm like water.

"Charlie! You're bleeding!"

"Ya think? Grab some towels."

Bob grabbed the towels and wrapped it around my hand. He was very attentive and very caring. I almost forgot about everything that had happened. Just kidding. Blood was dripping down my arm. I just didn't want to be mad at him.

"Wait here. I'll get my car," he said.

"But..."

"No buts. I need to get you to the ER," he said.

Bob walked out the door. I wasn't feeling so good. Bob better get back quick.

I didn't expect this to have happened.

Chapter Forty. Bob

I walked out to my car so Charlie wouldn't hear. As soon as I saw all the blood I knew it was more than just a superficial cut. It really looked like she severed a vein. Maybe even tendons. Best I call 911. They could assess and triage on the spot and could get here before I would be able to get her to the Outer Banks Hospital.

In the parking lot I pulled my phone out of my back pocket and dialed 911.

"Hello 911. What is your emergency?"

Trying to keep calm, I sputtered out, "Hi, I'm calling from Chuck's Grub & Tiki Bar on the Nags Head Pier. The owner, Charlie Foster, has cut herself pretty severely and requires immediate care. Can you please send out the paramedics?"

"Is she still conscious sir?"

"When I left to come outside she was, but she's losing blood pretty quickly. Please send someone now."

"Yes sir, I've already dispatched the squad. Their ETA is 2 minutes."

"Fine. I'll wait right here in the parking lot for them."

"Yes sir."

I hung up the phone and immediately heard the wailing of sirens. They were getting louder and louder with each passing second. It couldn't have been more than 90 seconds from my initial call before they pulled into the lot.

The paramedic riding shot gun, leapt from the squad before it came to a complete stop. He asked, "You the one who called?"

"Yes sir. It's Charlie. She's in here. Follow me!"

Both paramedics grabbed a couple of boxes. One, a communications system to talk to the hospital. The other, contained various medical supplies. They stacked those boxes on a gurney and followed me up the ramp to the restaurant entrance.

As they were getting everything together and running up the ramp, I explained to the paramedics that Charlie smashed her hand down on a broken beer bottle. Though she didn't realize it, I don't think, she also sliced her wrist in the process. Blood was pouring out much quicker than if it was just a palm of her hand that had been cut.

Once inside, we found Charlie slumped at the bar. "Bob, you didn't need to call 911." She said. "You could have just run me in to the hospital yourself."

"Charlie," one of the paramedics said, as he pushed me off to one side, "Charlie, I am Paramedic Thomas. How do you feel? Are you lightheaded at all?"

Charlie replied that she was.

As Paramedic Thomas was talking to Charlie, the other paramedic was on the communications system with the hospital. "This is Paramedic Aprile. We are At Chuck's Grub & Tiki Hut with a female patient, approximately in her early to mid-thirties. She is bleeding profusely and is claiming that she is lightheaded. Her breathing is rapid and shallow. Her skin is clammy and her pulse is weak."

The paramedic stopped talking. Apparently he was listening to instructions from the hospital. A few seconds later I heard, "Affirmative. The lips are blue, as are the fingernails."

Again there was quiet as Paramedic Aprile listened to instructions from the person at the other end of the line. All the while Paramedic Thomas was tying a tourniquet around Charlie's wrist. Thomas looked up at me and asked, "You sure this was an accident and not deliberate?"

"What is that supposed to mean?"

"I mean, the way the wrist is cut, it could be considered deliberate."

"No way! I was right here. She slammed her hand down on the bar and accidentally cut herself."

Just then I heard Paramedic Aprile say to the person on the other end of his communications, "10-4. Possible hypovolemic shock. Transporting immediately."

Aprile set down the phone and with a quick glance at Thomas they moved in unison. Years of working side by side allowed for non-communicative action as both men lifted Charlie simultaneously and hoisted her onto the gurney. Aprile strapped Charlie in and they wheeled her out to the squad. As they did, Thomas yelled to me over his shoulder, "meet us at the Outer Banks Hospital. I'm sure the police will want to ask you a few questions."

Panic now setting in, I closed the door to the restaurant and I tried to call Danny to come lock it up since I didn't have a key. No answer from Danny, which didn't exactly surprise me, so I left a message.

I ran to my Jeep and threw it into first gear, the back tires spinning for a moment before catching onto the blacktop beneath it. The squad already so far ahead that I couldn't see them. As I shifted into second gear, my phone rang.....

Chapter Forty-One. Danny

"Hey sausage guy. It's me, Danny, what be up?"

"Hey Danny. The paramedics just rushed Charlie to the Outer Banks Hospital and I need you to go over to the Tiki Bar and lock it up. I don't have a key."

"What they be takin' her to the hospital fer?"

"She cut her wrist pretty badly Danny. Look, I can't explain it all to you right now. I'm on my way to the hospital. Just please lock it up."

"Okay sausage guy. I'll find me a ride and git there as fast as I can."

"Thanks," Bob said as he clicked off the phone.

Chapter Forty-Two. Duffy Dixon

It was a pretty slow news night. So slow that I was thinking I would have to re-run the story about the Save Charlie's Campaign for the late news, when I heard the call for the squad to respond to Chuck's Grub & Tiki Hut. Not having much else to do I went out to the scene to see what all the fuss was about. Figuring it was nothing more than someone getting thrown from that damn mechanical shark, I didn't bring my camera crew.

I got there at about the time maintenance guy Danny pulled into the lot. I went over to his car and asked him what had happened.

"Don't rightly know. Hey! Wait! You're that news feller Dusty, ain't ya?"

"Duffy."

"Riiiight. Duffy. Now I remember."

"So you don't know what happened here then?"

"Not exactly. That sausage guy, he called and told me to git down here and lock up. Said Charlie cut her wrists and they rushed her to the hospital."

"Cut her wrists? Like on purpose?" I asked.

"Hmmmm. Bob, he didn't say so. Maybe, I guess."

"Mind if I have a look inside Danny?"

"Reckon it wouldn't hurt none."

I wasn't prepared to see what I saw. Broken glass on the bar with huge pools of blood on both the bar top and on the floor. Bloody towels were thrown off to the side. There was footprints and wheel marks, likely from the gurney, in the pools of blood. A real mess.

I immediately called the station and asked for my camera and sound guys to come on down. This would be our lead story for the late news.

"Danny. This is a big story. Would you mind hanging out here a bit and talk to me on camera?"

"Sure Dusty."

"Duffy."

"Oh yeah. Duffy."

It didn't take 10 minutes for my camera and sound crew to arrive from the television station. I set them up to the right of the bar. I had Danny stand on my left as I counted down the start of the story.

"3 - 2 - 1…..This is Duffy Dixon reporting for ABC 11. We're standing inside of Chuck's Grub & Tiki Hut on the Nags Head pier where it appears the bar owner Charlie Foster was severely injured. Standing with me is Danny, the maintenance guy for Chuck's…."

"That's Maintenance Dude, Dust…err, Duffy."

"Sorry. Now Danny, tell me, what happened here tonight?"

"Well, sir, I don't rightly know exactly. That sausage guy, he called me and said Charlie cut her wrists and they'd be haulin' her to the hospital."

"The sausage guy?"

"Yeah. That feller that come down from Ohio. Been hanging 'round here a coupla weeks now."

"As we reported earlier tonight, Charlie is mounting some sort of campaign to save her restaurant. She needed to raise $50,000. Danny, what kind of mood would you say Charlie has been in lately?"

"Well Duff. She been real tense lately. She's scared she's gonna lose this place. Didn't think she'd try this though…"

"Try what Danny?"

"You know. Try killin' herself."

"You're saying this was on purpose and not an accident Danny?"

"Don't know fer sure. Sure don't seem like no accident to me though."

"There you have it folks. Charlie Foster, who turned despondent from having to raise funds to save her Chuck's Grub & Tiki Bar attempted suicide here earlier this evening. More details as they become available. Reporting for ABC 11, This is Duffy Dixon."

….And we're clear!

Chapter Forty-Three. Charlie

I woke up in a hospital bed. The light was dim and there was a steady beeping coming from behind me. The door to my room quickly opened. "Good morning, Ms. Foster. My name is Betty and I am your nurse – at least for my shift." She giggled.

I looked down and saw the bandages around my wrist.

"You got yourself into quite a mess little lady," said Nurse Betty.

"What exactly happened? I remember when I cut my wrist but the rest is a little fuzzy."

"The doctor will be in shortly to discuss all the details. Rest up, dear."

She left just as quickly as she came. I laid there for awhile tapping my finger to the beeping of the machine behind me. I don't even remember how I got here. I was trying to concentrate and started dozing off...

I was startled awake.

"Good morning, Chuck. I am your doctor."

"Derek?"

He nodded his head yes. I totally forgot about my wrist. It wasn't that hard. I didn't remember much anyway.

"Wow. I can't believe it's you. I am in shock. How long has it been?" I asked.

"Since you actually went into shock last night or since we have seen each other?"

I tried to punch his shoulder. Pain shot through my arm. I was reminded why I was here in the first place.

"Charlie, listen. I need to get serious with you. How are you doing? I am a little worried about you."

"Derek-"

"It's Dr. Payne now." He quickly interrupted.

"HAHAHAHAHAHA! Stop it. You are not." I looked down at his name badge. It read: Derek Payne, MD. I couldn't help but start laughing again. "How did I forget that your last name is Payne?! I am blaming the pain meds."

"You aren't on any pain meds other than Tylenol 3. And those are just fluids." He was looking down at the clipboard, his right hand perched on his hip.

"Sorry, I'll shut up," I said.

Derek sat down on the edge of my bed. "Did you try to kill yourself?"

I felt my heart skip a beat. "No!"

"Are you sure?" He asked.

"Yes, I'm sure. I would never do that."

"What about the restaurant? That was your father's place. You can admit to being stressed. It's okay." He said.

"I know I'm stressed. How do you think I cut myself in the first place? I slammed a beer bottle down while venting. I don't need a pretty boy doctor to tell me I'm stressed."

"I wasn't trying to—"

"Tell me what is in here." I held up the bed pan to his face.

"Nothing," he said.

"That's right. No shit, Sherlock."

He stormed out of the room. I thought it was kind of clever. Why in the world do I have a bed pan anyway? My legs work just fine. Dr. Payne opened the door and slammed a newspaper down on my lap. "You can joke all you want but this is what the world thinks."

I picked up the paper. The headline read: CHARLIE FOSTER RUSHED TO HOSPITAL AFTER APPARENT SUICIDE ATTEMPT.

"Dere- I mean Dr. Payne. How in the world did this happen? How did the newspapers find out? Who told them this?"

KNOCK. KNOCK. KNOCK.

"Excuse me, Doctor. Charlie has a visitor. Bob Evans," said Nurse Betty.

Derek turned and looked at me. "Did you order food?"

Chapter Forty-Four. Bob

"Hi Doc." I said. "Can I talk to you for a minute?"

"Sure….."

"Out in the hallway here…"

Dr Payne glanced back at Charlie who was drifting back to sleep. "She's gonna be out of it most of the day. The Tylenol 3 will keep her sedated pretty good. But if you want to go out in the hallway, sure, we can do that. Just for a minute. I have other patients to check in on."

"Thanks Doc."

Looking up and down the hall to make sure no one else was within earshot, I began.

"Tell me doc. How is she?"

"Well. Bob, is it?"

"Yeah, Bob."

"Bob, I can only release information to family, especially in this type of case."

"What type of case is that?"

"Attempted suicide Bob."

Thinking for moment, I don't even know how it happened. I just reacted and blurted out, "I'm her cousin. Cousin Bob."

"Excuse me Bob, but I've known Charlie since first grade. We went to Manteo elementary, middle and high schools together. Even dated once. I don't remember a cousin Bob."

"Yeah, I'm cousin Bob from Ohio. We didn't visit often. But I'm down here now helping Charlie work out her restaurant problem."

"Ok Bob. Reckon I'll take your word for it since Charlie doesn't have any other immediate family here. Someone is going to have to know."

"Know what?" I asked.

"Well, Bob, when it's apparent that there was an attempted suicide, by law I am required to hold Charlie over for observation. Just to be sure she's ok."

"Hold her over for observation?"

"Yes. We'll take her to TPI, er, that's Tidewater Psychiatric Institute." Licensed psychiatrists will talk to her. See what her frame of mind is, and make whatever determination they have to make."

"But I was there when she injured herself. It was nothing more than an accident."

"You say accident Bob, but do you know for sure what was going on in her mind?"

"Yes, she's been upset over the whole restaurant possibly going out of business."

"Right! She was upset…."

"As anyone would be!" I exclaimed.

"Right, as anyone would be. But then she has these cut wrists. You don't know what was going on in her head. I don't know what was going on in her head. Realistically, Charlie may not have know what was going on in her head."

Rage was now filling my body and I exploded at the doctor. "What does THAT mean?" I asked, spitting out "that" with as much venom as I could muster.

"That means it may have been done unconsciously. Charlie may not have known what she was doing in that instant. She may have acted purely on instinct."

I had nothing to say to that. Clearly Dr Payne knows more about this type of thing than I do. I mean, I sell orthopedic flip-flops for God sakes. What do I know?

"Well doc, how long will this observation be?'

"Generally the law stipulates that it's at least 48 hours. But based on the psychiatrists' opinion, it could be longer."

"Will they allow visitors?"

"Not within the initial 48 hours I'm afraid."

"Ok doc. I appreciate that. Mind if I go in and see her now?"

"Sure. Likely she'll just be sleeping the rest of the day. They'll be transporting her to TPI tonight."

"Thank you doctor."

"Keep good thoughts Cousin Bob." Winking as he said the word "cousin."

I walked into Charlie's room and sat with her for a couple of hours just watching her sleep.

——-

It was just before lunch when my cell phone rang. When I saw the number, my stomach fell to my feet. I went out into the hallway to answer it.

"Hello?"

"Hey Bob Evans, still making the sausages or what?

"Yeah, good one. As always boss. What's up?"

"Well Bob, my boy, our orthopedic flip-flop sales are slipping a great deal. Corporate is threatening to pull the line out of production. Now, I know you have about 3 years worth of vacation to use up, but was kinda wonderin' when we might see you burnin' those sales phone lines again? No one can sell an orthopedic flip-flop like you. Plus you had that big nursing home account on the hook, all you had to do was reel them in. But then you left abruptly for your vacation."

Damn! Up to this point I hadn't thought about whether I was gonna stay here on the Outer Banks permanently, or gather Bruno up and head back to real life in Ohio. I did promise Charlie that I'd help her raise the $50,000 needed to save the restaurant. But am I able to offer her the help if I'm here not working, or there working and making a paycheck every week? Collecting that commission on the nursing home account would certainly go along way toward that $50 Gs.

"Hey Sausage, you still there?"

"Uh, yeah, boss. Just thinkin'."

"Don't think too long. I need you back up here by end of next week. We have a huge marketing campaign to kick off for these flip-flops."

"Yeah, boss. I'll be in touch…."

With that I disconnected the phone and went back into Charlie's room for a few more hours. All the while she never woke.

Finally around 4 that afternoon I left the hospital as the orderlies prepared Charlie for the ride to Tidewater.

Chapter Forty-Five. Charlie

It had only been one day but my stay at the Holy Water Hotel – I can't remember the name but it somehow seems appropriate for the exorcising of demons -- had been interesting. The room was sterile and boring. I am still not sure how I ended up here. How did a cut from a beer bottle turn into this?

There was a knock on my door. It was Dr. Stankovich. "Charlie, I've looked over your file and our admissions interview, I honestly don't see why you can't go home today. You do not pose a threat to yourself or others," said Dr. Stankovich.

"So I can go home today?"

"I'm working on it. The protocol states two days but as I said before, there is no reason for you to be here," He said. "I will be back with an update."

"Thanks," I said as he slipped out the door.

More waiting. One thing I have learned about the medical community, they run their business like they have nothing but time. I needed to use the restroom so I poked my head out of the door to let someone know. I also wanted to see if Dr. Stankovich was around. I turned the corner and saw him talking with someone. I sat down in the corner to wait for him to finish. I couldn't quite see who he was talking to but the conversation seemed to be a difficult one. Dr. Stankovich had a file in his hand that he kept flipping through. A piece of paper fell out; he bent down to pick it up. It was JOE!

No way. I didn't want him to see me. Why was he here? Why was he talking to Dr. Stankovich. Was that my file? I wanted to confront Joe but I knew better. I tried to get closer so I could hear what they were saying when I felt someone grab my arm. My heart jumped and my body got tense. Then I felt my wrist. "Ouch," I yelled.

"What are you doing out here, dear?" It was one of the nurses.

"I just needed to pee," I said.

"The bathroom is over here. Let's go sweetie."

I couldn't remember her name but something about her screamed Aunt Bee. She took me to the bathroom – you have to be supervised when you pee in the joint – then she brought me back to my room. I didn't have a good feeling about Joe. Something seemed off. Why would he be here?

Two-and-half hours went by when there was finally a knock on the door. The door opened. "Charlie?" It was Dr. Stankovich. "Unfortunately, I have some bad news," he said.

I could see where this was going.

"You will have to stay one more day before we can discharge you."

"Why?" I asked.

"They won't let me skip protocol on this one," he said.

"But they have in the past?"

"Well..uh..see..um.." He was clearly dancing around something.

"Spit it out, doc."

"We have follow protocol. Sorry." He left abruptly.

Freakin' Joe. I knew that guy was a turd wagon.

Chapter Forty-Six. Charlie

It was finally time to leave. It's amazing how two days can feel like a month in a place like this. Aunt Bee came in the room and got me ready for discharge. It will be nice to pee again without someone looking over my shoulder. Dr. Stankovich came in for the final discharge. "Congratulations, Charlie, you are finally out of here."

"Thanks, warden." He laughed, but I wasn't joking.

"You'll be fine, Charlie. Good luck," he said.

Aunt Bee came back in, "Your ride is here, Charlie."

"Who is picking me up?" I asked.

Dr. Stankovich looked at his clipboard. "Looks like Robert Evans."

Hearing the name Robert made me giggle. I don't know why but he didn't seem like a Robert. I mean, I know Bob comes from Robert but still, I feel like he isn't a Robert. I sat in the discharge area waiting for Bob. His car pulled up. I ran to the door.

"BOB! I mean ROBERT! It's the sausage guy!!" I hugged him as he walked toward me. He hugged me back. I liked the way it felt – warm and safe. I wanted to stay there.

"It's so good to see you, Charlie. I've been so worried," Bob said. "I brought some clothes for you."

"Great. I will change in the car." Bob looked a little surprised. "I don't want to be here anymore."

"No problem" he said.

I changed in car while Bob stood outside. "Hey Robert, you didn't happen to grab a pair of shoes, did you?"

"It's Bob, and yes, I did." He opened the back and grabbed a box. "They are just your size."

"New shoes?" I was impressed until I saw what they were. "Orthopedic Flip-Flops?"

"Hey, take what you can get. That's for calling me Robert."

I threw a flip-flop at him. I ended up putting them on. It was either the flip-flops or the dumb socks from the Holy Water Jail.

Bob and I didn't say much at first. I had so much I wanted to say but I wasn't sure how to say it. Bob finally spoke.

"I'm really glad you are okay." He put his hand on my leg as he said it. I put my hand on his. I felt a rush of emotion go through my body, "I'm really glad you are here. I can't thank you enough for…everything." I started to tear up a bit. Bob stopped the car and pulled over to the side of the road. He wiped a tear from my eye and started to hug me. Then our lips touched. I'm not sure who kissed whom but I didn't care. His lips were soft and forgiving. It was just like I imagined, except for the dumb flip-flops and the fact that he picked me up from a nut house. For a moment it felt like we were the only ones in the world.

Then Bob's phone rang. "It's just my cousin, Joe. I will call him back. I reckon I should get you back home."

We drove back to the restaurant. The closer we got, the more it felt like reality was setting in. Bob opened the door to the restaurant to let me in. Without thinking I blurted out, "I think Joe is up to something."

"Joe? What would make you think that?"

"I saw him at the nut house yesterday. Dr. Stankovich was going to discharge me early then I saw Joe talking to him. It was after their conversation that I was kept for another day."

"Charlie, I don't think Joe is smart enough to pull something like that off."

"I have never fully trusted that guy. I am telling you he is up to no good. Promise me you'll do some digging for me. My entire life is depending on it.

Bob put his hand on my shoulder. I pulled him closer. "I will see what I can find. You know I would do anything for you," said Bob.

"I know." In the midst of this crap storm, somehow, I think I am falling for him. And these flip-flops are actually kind of comfortable. "Thanks, Bob.

Chapter Forty-Six. Joe

"Yeah, I think keeping that ukulele playing bitch in the loony bin for that extra 24 hours helped us get the marketing plan together," I said into my phone. "Yeah, yeah, don't worry. This is gonna work. You can count on me."

I clicked off the call and slipped my cell phone into the back left pocket of my khakis. "Now to get that damn cousin of mine off the trail for a bit," I muttered under my breath.

I reached into the refrigerator and grabbed a Kitty Hawk Blonde beer. Opening the bottle, I took a long sip from it as I heard the crunch of gravel beneath the tires of a car in the driveway. Looking out the front window I saw Bob's Jeep.

Time to put the second act of my plan into place, I thought.

A few seconds later Bob came through the front door, noticed the beer in my hand and asked if I minded if he had one too. I motioned toward the refrigerator.

Opening his bottle and throwing the cap onto the counter, Bob asked, "So cuz, what did you do the last coupla days?

"Nothing exciting. I had some work I needed to attend to. Stuff like that. Let us not forget, not all of us are on vacation."

"By chance, did your business bring you up to Tidewater yesterday at all?"

Wondering why Bob brought that up, I decided I better be careful as to how I responded to his question. After a second or two, I simply said, "No. I'm a county worker. No need for me to have gone to Virginia." Saying it as confidently as I could.

Bob took a pull from his beer, set it down on the coffee table and then fell heavily onto the couch.

"Why would you ask me that Bob?"

"Well, I was up at TPI to pick up Charlie a little bit ago and she said she saw you there yesterday. Were you there Joe?"

"No I wasn't there! I told you that already! What's with the 3rd degree anyway?"

"I don't know cuz. She just seemed real positive that you were there for some reason."

"Bob…..now you know I like Charlie. Hell, I've been trying to work with both you and her to solve this whole restaurant thing, so don't take this the wrong way, I mean, who you gonna believe? Someone in the psych ward, or your own flesh and blood?"

"Ok Joe. Sorry I even brought it up. I guess there is no real reason why you would be there."

I wasn't sure at all that Bob really believed me, so I figured it best to change the subject and try diverting Bob's attention to something else.

Taking a seat in the chair opposite where Bob was sitting on the couch I said, "Hey not sure if your boss got hold of you or not, but he left a message on my home voicemail here. Said he needed you back in Ohio to close some big deal and prop the orthopedic flip-flop division back up. What's that all about?"

"Yeah. I talked to him. Seems like the place can't survive without me. I leave for a few weeks and an entire line of shoes crashes and burns."

"Must be nice to be needed….."

"Not really. Just piling up work on one guy so they don't have to pay another one."

"So what's the plan then Bobby?" A noticeable frown crossed his face when I said the name "Bobby." Only the family calls him that and he hates it. Only hates being called Robert even worse.

"I don't know yet Joey." Bob emphasizing "Joey" in a mocking fashion. "There is a lot to consider at the moment. On one hand, this seems like the absolute worst time for me to pick up and head back to Ohio with Charlie being as vulnerable as she is. Plus, I think we are on the path to being more than just friends."

"And on the other hand?" I asked.

"Well, as you know, Charlie still needs to raise the $50,000 for her part of the pier and I promised to help any way I could. It seems staying here and not being back in Ohio making commissions to put toward that debt doesn't seem smart either. I don't want to leave, but that does seem like the best way to raise the money. What do you think Joe?"

I got up and went back to the kitchen and grabbed us two more Kitty Hawk Blondes, giving one to Bob. Knowing that this was the exact opening I needed to get my cousin off the Outer Banks for a while.

"I would never just come out to tell you what to do dear cousin, but since you asked...."

"I did ask. I need some clarity in this Joe. I feel I'm too close to Charlie, to the restaurant, to the pier, to the whole damn thing. I need someone's advice that isn't ass-deep into it like I am."

"Ok, Bob, but only because you asked."

"I did."

"Ok. Well, I think you're doing no good here. You're not doing Charlie any good. You're not doing yourself any good. Poor Charlie needs a clear head to figure out her future, and I fear you're clouding her judgment right now. She's thinking too much about you rather than what she needs to do to raise this money. She doesn't have an infinite amount of time on this you know."

"Yeah, I know Joe." Bob said, now looking down at his feet. He slowly replied, "So you think I should head back home and to my job." Bob phrased it as a statement, rather than as a question.

"Yes, I do. Get that commission from that account that you're working on. Close that deal since most of the work is already done, and bring that check back here to the Outer Banks to help Charlie out."

"But Joe, I can't…..I mean, I don't know if I should leave Charlie with her state of mind being what it is."

"Bob, we're family. I'll tell you what. I'll keep an eye on Charlie. I'll make sure she's ok so you won't have to worry about her while you're gone."

"Well, it won't be for more than a month. I can close that deal, grab my check, officially quit my job and be back down in 5 weeks at the most. Maybe even sooner."

"See? Not so bad cuz."

"No, guess not."

Bob finished his beer, got up and said, "Thanks for being a sounding board Joe. I reckon I better call my boss to let him know I'll be back in a couple of days. I'll drive all day tomorrow and be back at my desk the next day. Reckon I better let Charlie know too. I'm gonna run over to the Tiki Bar to let her know, then I'll be back to pack."

"The most sensible thing you could do" I replied. "And oh, by the way, don't forget to take Boris the cat with you."

Both men laughed as Bob scampered down the stairs to his Jeep in the driveway. I reached into my back left pocket and grabbed my cell phone....

"Yeah, it's me. Told you I'd take care of it. We should be able to move in for the kill in the next couple of days......Yeah, yeah, he's out of the way for now. Probably for the next month or so. Plenty of time for our plan to come together...."

Chapter Forty-Seven. Charlie

Sunday morning could not have come at a better time. Somehow Danny kept the restaurant going while I was away. The place was a little messy but I had no room to complain. I had the day to not only clean up the restaurant, but clean up myself. It was early morning; I had missed the sunrise but seeing the sun bounce off the ocean water brought joy to my heart. I fixed a cup of coffee and took it out on the balcony. I could feel the salty ocean air around me; a morning has never been so perfect. The steam coming off the cup of coffee made me feel cozy as my hair blew in the perfect ocean breeze.

My phone rang. It was Jamie. What in the world does she want? Jamie calls for two things: money and gossip. Lord knows I don't have any money.

I answered the phone, "Hello."

"Hey. I need to talk to you. Can I come over?"

"Sure," I said. "Is everything okay?"

"I don't know. I will explain when I get there."

"Sure." I hung up the phone. Now I was worried.

Jamie pulled in the parking lot a few minutes later. I unlocked the door to let her in. She looked disheveled. Let's be honest, she always looks disheveled, but now she looked a little more than usual. She was tired and stressed. Before I had a chance to talk she started rambling.

"Chuck, I don't even know where to begin."

She was pacing back and forth in front of the bar. Her hands were waving around wildly.

"Chuck, I need to tell you some things and what I need for you to do is just listen."

I was worried.

"Are you listening, Chuck?"

I nodded my head yes.

"Then say something."

"I didn't know if I was allowed to." I finally spoke half laughing at the production she was putting on.

"It's not funny."

"I'm sorry, Jamie. I know, It's not funny. I'm listening. But hold on real quick." I went into my studio and grabbed a mug that said I'M LISTENING and came back in the room. "Okay, I'm ready."

Jamie came over to the bar where I was sitting and grabbed both of my hands. "Chuck, I appreciate your sarcastic wit, but this isn't the time."

I didn't know what to say. I don't think anyone has ever called me out like that. I am actually kind of amazed.

"Chuck. Listen. I am in trouble and so are you."

How the hell was I in trouble, besides the obvious.

"Roy is not happy."

Who the hell is Roy? Then I realized I wasn't speaking out loud. "Who the hell is Roy?"

"My boyfriend. Try to keep up."

I still don't remember Roy.

"I was here the past couple of days helping Danny with your restaurant. He was getting real swamped and called me in a panic. I came to help but I didn't tell Roy."

Roy was still not ringing a bell.

"He came here and saw me here with Danny and…"

"Jamie, did you two do something?"

"No. But we were close. Maybe closer than we should have been."

"Is that what this is about? You and Roy?"

"It gets worse," she said. Joe was here too. He knew you weren't here."

"Joe?"

"Yeah, Joe. And he was showing some people around. It was like he was trying to get someone to buy it or something."

My interest was definitely piqued. Although I wasn't entirely surprised with what I saw at Shady Pines when I was there. He is definitely up to something. I think my original instincts on the turd wagon were correct.

I muttered out a "h-m-m."

"I don't trust the guy, Chuck. He comes to Lucky 12 all the time. He has some shady conversations."

"Like what?" I asked.

"I'm pretty sure he watches you on your webcams."

"What?"

"Yeah. One time I heard him talking about watching you and then he saw the shark attack and called 911 or something. I'm not totally sure but I wouldn't be surprised if he didn't somehow, in some crazy way, plan for all of this to happen."

I stood there shocked. To think of someone watching me. I never liked the idea of the webcams but I did it because I was told I had to by – JOE.

"Oh my goodness, Jamie. You are often very flighty and have no clue what you are talking about but this time I think you are on to something, my sweet cousin. Joe started all of this. I can't believe it. It's all Joe."

"What about Bob?" She interrupted.

"Great movie."

"No, I mean do you think Bob has anything to do with it? He showed up when all of this went down?"

All of this was too much for me to think about. Sure. Joe. But Bob? It couldn't be Bob, right? I didn't have time to think about it. A very tall, muscular man was charging up the steps of the restaurant and headed for the front door.

"I think I remember Roy."

Chapter Forty-Eight. Charlie

Roy charged up the steps and opened the door. Veins were popping out of his neck and forearms.

"I'm sure this is going to be fine," I said.

"Roy want Jamie. Roy beat up Danny." I am sure it sounded more intelligent than that but under the circumstances I am allowed to make him sound dumb.

Jamie stood in the corner and I was behind the bar. I could tell Jamie didn't know what to do. There was a tear in Roy's eye.
I giggled, "Are you crying? Over Jamie? Dude, I don't know if you know this but…"

Jamie threw a bar towel and hit me in the face. "Ouch." It didn't hurt as much as smell really weird.

"Alright, enough is enough. Roy you need to talk this out with Jamie. Who knows where the hell Danny is…probably at Lucky 12 looking for Jamie." As soon as it came out of my mouth I wished I could take it right back. If Roy's eyes could turn red they would have. He slammed his fists down on the table and knocked over the ketchup bottle.

"Hey, you watch it, that's my grandma's ketchup bottle."

Roy stopped and picked it up. "Really?"

"It's a ketchup bottle, dude. No." I snapped back.

Roy threw the bottle on the floor and headed in Jamie's direction. I wasn't sure what to do. Then the door opened. Now who? It was Bob. Roy stopped in his tracks. He turned around, "You're the little twerp that was with Danny that night. You brought him to see Jamie."

Bob looked like he needed to change his panties. Yes, his panties. Roy charged toward Bob and then tripped over the ketchup bottle. His flip-flops flew off his feet. One landed on the shark and the other in the overhead fan. Roy laid there for a second. Bob walked over and patted him on the back. "You know I can set you up with a real nice pair of supportive flip-flops. On the house." Bob said.

Roy looked up a little embarrassed over the stunt he pulled.

Jamie finally spoke, "you okay, Roy?"

"Yeah, I'm fine," he said. "Sorry to come charging into your restaurant Chuck. I just miss Jamie so bad. When I heard she was here, I knew she had to be with Danny."

"I'm just helping Chuck out, Roy. You have to stop being so jealous. Go home and we can talk about this tomorrow."

Roy shook his head and looked at Bob, "How 'bout those flip-flops?

"Sure," Bob said. "I'll meet you outside. I just need to talk to Chuck real quick.

Roy waved as if to say that's fine and walked out the door.

Jamie headed for the bar and cracked open a Weeping Radish Corolla Gold.

"Can I talk to you alone?" He said.

"Sure." We headed into my studio for a little one on one time. There is just something about Bob that puts me at ease. His face wasn't relaxed though. He looked full of worry.

"I've missed you." I said.

Bob smiled. "I need to talk to you about something." He said.

"Okay, you know you can talk to me about anything." I was a little worried where this was headed.

Bob looked down at his feet and then back up at me. "My boss called and needs me to come back to close a big deal."

I felt my throat tighten up like I was having some sort of allergic reaction. "Go back where? Ohio?"

Bob shook his head. "Yes, Ohio."

"But you hate it there."

"I know, but I would be doing it for you. Joe even thinks it's a good idea."

"Don't get me started on Joe. He is the whole reason I am in this mess," I said. Bob looked at me a little perplexed. "Yeah, the man I thought was the enemy is the enemy. He wants me to lose this place. He's trying to sell it out from under me."

"Joe would never do that," said Bob.

"Are you in on it, too?" I asked.

"That's crazy! I'm trying to help you."

"Have you been watching me too?"

Bob looked stunned he didn't know what to say.

"What? Does Boris have your tongue? I should have known you would screw me over with your dumb flip-flops and stupid cat."

Then there was a quick knock on the door. "Hey guys." It was Roy. "I heard you say something about flip-flops? Mine are still broken."

"Can you hold it for a second, Roy?" Bob asked.

"No, It's okay. You go give your dumb flip-flops to Roy. When you're finished you can point your car north and head back where you belong."

"It's not like that," said Bob. "I'm doing this for you."

"We'll see about that," I said.

I watched Bob walk out. I didn't want him to go. He did belong here. I looked down at my feet and was reminded that I was wearing a pair of those dumb flip-flops. They are comfortable. I was startled away from my thoughts when Danny barged through the back studio door.

"What's up, Chuck?" He laughed stupidly. "That never gets old."

"Keep it in your pants and take down all the cameras."

I grabbed my paddleboard and headed for my happy place. Maybe Mother Ocean would have some advice.

Chapter Forty-Nine. Bob

I hit the Capitol Beltway around Washington DC at about noon on my way back to Cleveland. The 5 hour drive going by in one huge blur. I had been completely lost in thought. The horn blast of the big rig that I accidentally just cut off suddenly startled me back to reality.

All I had been able to think about was having to leave Charlie at one of the most vulnerable points in her life. Would my departure adversely affect any relationship that seems to have been budding very recently? Or will it strengthen it? You know, that absence making the heart grow fonder BS. Surely she had to believe that me going back to get that commission would be the best thing for her. She would see that as an act of support rather than abandonment. Right?

My heart felt one way, but my brain seemed to steer me in another direction.

I made my way off the Beltway and onto I-270, continuing on my trek north and west toward the Buckeye state when my cell phone rang. It was Joe.

I pressed the phone button on the Jeep steering wheel. Thank goodness for Bluetooth, I thought…..

"Hey Joe." I said into the speaker.

"Hey cuz," Joe replied back. "How's the trip? Should be around Washington I would figure 'bout now."

"Yeah. Just hit Maryland a minute ago." I replied.

"Cool. Cool. Just making sure everything was good."

"That's it?" I asked.

"Yep. Thanks it." Joe responded. "Be safe. Let me know when you make it back home."

"Um, ok Joe. I will."

I pressed the hang up button on the steering wheel.

That was weird, I thought. It almost felt like Joe was checking up on me to make sure I really had left the Outer Banks.

A few more miles up the road, I convinced myself that, no, Joe was just being family and wanted to know that the drive was going ok. I think......

I switched from listening to Vos and Bonnie's "My Wife Hates Me" podcast over to the Steve Forbert Pandora station. The American in Me was playing:

"The off ramp backed up miles today
And the carbon fumes
Were drifting towards the sky
The sky began to cry
And the thunder booms."

I continued onto I-70 and was driving alongside of the mountain leading into Breezewood, Pennsylvania. I love this part of the drive, looking down to see that little white church in the valley. It reminds me of Mayberry, the fictional town from the Andy Griffith Show. Peaceful, beautiful. I could picture Andy, Opie and Aunt Bee going into that church on a Sunday.

Again, I was startled back to reality by Bob Marley's "No woman, No Cry" ring tone on my cell phone. It was Joe again.

"Hey Joe, what's up now?"

"Hey Bob. Sorry to bother you again. Thinking about this Chuck situation and her buying the pier. How much do you think your commission will be on that nursing home account?"

"I don't know exactly Joe, pretty significant I would guess. Why?" I asked.

"Just checking to see if you guys would have enough for the purchase price with just that, is all."

"Well, I can't say really. But between that, Charlie winning the uke contest, and me cashing in some of my 401k, I would think we'd have enough to cover."

There was a long pause on the other end of the phone. Finally Joe replied, "......and you think you'd be back with the cash in about a month?"

"If I had to guess Joe, that would be the timeline," I replied.

Ok. Cool. I figured as much. Just wanted to be sure. Well, be safe on the rest of your drive," Joe said before hanging up the phone.

I don't know exactly what it was, but now Joe had the hair standing up on the back of my neck. All of a sudden, he certainly seemed to be very inquisitive as to exact dollar figures and timelines.

A few minutes later, and a few more miles down the road, I pulled into the Exxon Gateway Travel Plaza in Breezewood. I jumped out of the Jeep, leaving my cell phone sitting in the cup holder while I pumped gas and went inside to use the bathroom, and to get another cup of coffee for the homestretch part of my drive. Jumping back into the Jeep, I cranked the radio to Steve Forbert's "Goin' Down to Laurel" as I threw the Jeep into first gear, then 2nd, 3rd and 4th, as I pulled back into traffic and onto the Pennsylvania Turnpike, all the while not noticing I had a voicemail from Charlie on my phone.

Chapter Fifty. Joe

"I told you that I didn't want to be seen with you. Not now anyway!" George said to me.

George, you might remember, was one of the initial investors that I had brought together at the meeting with Mike and Randi, the Nags Head pier owners at the Comfort Inn. He thought the asking price of $5 million was outrageous. Turns out, as I first thought, he was just trying to throw everyone off his scent. He did indeed want the pier for himself.

"George, just take a deep breath and settle down. No one is going to put 2 and 2 together and figure out that we're calling an audible on this pier thing. Anyone seeing us here is just going to think it's two old friends having a cup of coffee together. Nothing more." I replied.

"Just the same, I didn't get to be successful by being stupid. This won't be good for either of us if our plot is discovered. Surely even you realize that Joe."

"It's fine George. No one is paying attention to us anyway." I said, trying to reassure him. "Now, our plan is starting to come together. Just relax." I said.

"So you assure me that you've fixed it so that brat girl won't raise the money in time?"

"Yes George. I said I would. But you just remember the other two important factors. You need to raise your capital before that nosey buttinski cousin of mine gets back next month. And even more importantly, you remember to pay me that 10% finders fee on the purchase price if you end up with the pier."

"Yeah, 10% of $5 million buys you a lot of tall Pabst Blue Ribbons, doesn't it Joe?"

I shot George a dirty look. And I truly hope he noticed it too. "Just don't you worry about what I'm spending my half mill on. You just worry about holding up your end of the bargain."

It was at this point that I wondered if I had sold my soul to the devil. George was a successful business man, that's true, but he was also a world class jerk. No one likes to have to deal with him.

Just then out of the corner of my eye, I saw someone approach our table.

"Hey boys, planning on world domination this morning?"

It was Duffy Dixon from ABC 11. He stopped in for a cup of coffee.

"Yeah, good one Dixon," George said. "Slow news day for you? Maybe I should buy that crap station of yours and hire someone that really knows how to do the news."

"Ah, just as pleasant as always George," Duffy replied. He grabbed his to go coffee and made his way back out the door while saying over his shoulder, "Just be careful George, even snakes have a way of getting killed too."

Turning his icy gaze back at me, George spit out, "See? I told you we shouldn't be seen together. People might start drawing some conclusions, especially the nosey types."

"You know what George?" I said. "I'm tired of your company anyway. You just remember those two things you need to take care of. I'll be in touch."

With that, I asked for a to go cup for my coffee and made my way out into the brilliant sunlight of the Outer Banks.

Chapter Fifty-One. Duffy

Setting my coffee down on my desk, it occurred to me that there seemed to be a little bit more to that meeting between Joe and George this morning. I don't know what. Maybe it is just a slow news day and I'm trying to make something out of nothing. I don't know. But still.....

"Whatcha got going on this morning Duff? Anything?" Asked Fred Midgette, station manger of ABC 11, as he busted into my cubicle.

"Not sure Skip." I replied. I always called my bosses Skip. That way I never really had to learn their names. Station Managers come and go. I come and go. Who needs the hassle?

"Well, Duff, we have a newscast to get on the air at 6 tonight. We need something. You can't just keep doing feature stories on the people of the Outer Banks. The viewers need some hard hitting news from time to time to keep their interest."

"Yeah, Skip. I may have something. Just don't know yet. I need to make some phone calls first."

I took a long slurp of my now lukewarm coffee and reached for my phone and started dialing, signaling it was time for Fred to leave. I called the county offices. I called Mike and Randi. I called Kirk Bashnagel. I even called Ollie Frakingham….I mean Farkingham. Why couldn't he be like those other Hollywood movie types and just change his name to something easy like Smith or Simon or something? I smelled some sort of story here that has to do with George and Joe this morning. George seemed too cagey and even more belligerent than usual. Almost like he's trying to scare me away. I may not have the story by the 6pm broadcast. But I'll get it. Oh, I'll get it. That much you can count on….

Chapter Fifty-Two. Charlie

"Okay, Chuck. Cameras are done," Danny said. He was still on the ladder and apparently very proud of himself.

"By done you mean that they are down, correct?" This was non-negotiable.

"Well, shit. No. But they ain't on."

"I want them down. In the trash. Out of here." I said.

"I ain't got time for that right now, Chuck. I got places to be," Danny said.

"Just make sure it gets done soon," I said.

I went over to the bar to stock a new shipment of Stumpy Point Ale, Kill Devil Scotch Ale and Hatteras Red that just came in from the Lost Colony Brewery. My phone rang. I didn't recognize the number so I sent it to voicemail. The phone rang again -- same number. I pushed it to voicemail again and put it in my back pocket. The phone rang again.

"Just answer the damn phone, Chuck." Yelled Danny.

I took the phone out of my pocket – same number. I was afraid to answer. It was either bad news or a nut job.

"Hello?"

"Hi, is this Charlie Foster?"

"Yes?"

"This is Duffy Dixon from-"

"I remember who you are."

"I have some interesting news regarding the pier. Can you meet me at The Front Porch Cafe in Nags Head in a half hour?" Duffy asked.

"Sure."

I hung up the phone. I had goose bumps.

"Who the hell was that?" Asked Danny.

"Oh. Umm, wrong number." At this point I wasn't sure who I could trust. "I need to run some errands. I will be back later. You can lock up on your way out."

I hopped on my bike and headed for the coffee shop. When I got there the place was moderately busy. Lots of laptops. Lots of people trying to look important. I ordered my usual, the cinnamon and vanilla latte. I took a seat by the window. Duffy walked up a few minutes later.

"Hey Charlie, let's sit outside. There are a few too many ears in here.

Duffy grabbed a coffee and met me outside on the patio. "You are probably wondering why I called you here today."

"Yep."

"I have been on the phone nearly all morning and I think I am onto something with this pier situation," Duffy said.

I could feel my chest tighten. Duffy continued.

"I ran into Joe and George earlier this morning. I overheard them talking about the pier. From what I have gathered, they are in cahoots to buy the pier. I think Joe is getting a pay out or something. I am still figuring some things out."

Things were starting to make sense. I didn't say much.

"You don't seem that surprised," said Duffy.

"I'm not. I heard from one of the waitresses at Lucky 12 that she overheard something similar from Joe one night. He was even taking investors around the restaurant while I was gone."

"No kidding." Duffy was writing furiously in his notebook. "I'm going on the air with this. I'm not sure exactly how I'm going to piece it all together but I think we have to go public with this."

"Are you sure? Don't you think it might be better to investigate this a little further before you take it public?"

"I don't know. I do know this is corrupt. There is more to this than meets the eye. I'm not sure how deep it goes but I am going to find out."

Duffy seemed incredibly confident. It gave me some hope. Duffy stood up from the table and shook my hand. "We just might save your restaurant after all."

I shook his hand and watched as he walked away. I needed to call Bob. Why wasn't he answering his phone?

Chapter Fifty-Three. Bob

"You're going to wake up in your town
But we'll be scheduled to appear
A thousand miles away from here."

I love singing at the top of my lungs with Jackson Browne "as the miles roll away," down the Pennsylvania Turnpike. With the windows down and the truckers seemingly every other vehicle on the road, no one can hear my warbling. Which is good, because I am a terrible singer.

On the turnpike, the hills gave way to valleys, which gave way to twists and turns in the road. All of a sudden that coffee I grabbed in Breezewood, about 80 miles back, is wanting to get out. Luckily I saw that big blue sign on the side of the road that brought welcome relief to my situation. "Rest Area - 2 miles."

I pulled the Jeep into a parking spot at the rest area, rolled up the windows and grabbed my phone to see what texts or emails I may have missed while driving. As I got out from behind the wheel of the Jeep and started for the front door of the rest area, I saw a missed voicemail from Charlie.

The voicemail was simple and to the point. All it said was to call ASAP.

Forgetting my bladder for a moment, and by the way, isn't it funny that you may have to go to the bathroom really bad, but something comes up and then interrupts that thought process? This made me not feel like it was a dire emergency to get into the men's room, so I hit redial.

Ring…..ring……ring……Voicemail. Great, playing phone tag, I thought.

"Hey Charlie. Got your message. Just calling back. Should be back in Ohio in the next coupla hours. Call me back."

I slipped the phone into one of the pockets in my cargo shorts and headed toward the building to readdress my bladder situation.

Chapter Fifty-Four. Duffy Dixon

You know? It's ridiculous the way this newsroom runs sometimes, I thought to myself. First Skip wants a hard news story. Then he cans it. Says there's no corroborating evidence to what I've got on the Joe/George angle on the pier. Says he's worried about the station getting sued for libel or something. That's the problem with those that make it into management, they become soft. They don't remember what it's like to go out and unearth a great story. And that's what I did here. I unearthed a great story. Friggin' station manager can kiss my rear end for all I care. He wants more evidence? I'll get him more evidence.

I thought about this story all afternoon. I figured the best way to get something is to have some sort of stooge go and talk to George and Joe independently. Someone who would wear a wire to record the conversations. I couldn't do it. Being a reporter, people get to be very guarded as to what they say around me. They're not as free with information. No, what I need is someone so, oh, what's the word I'm looking for? Someone so, I don't know, benign, I guess. Someone who wouldn't pose any sort of threat because no one would expect them to be able to put 2 and 2 together. But who? Who can I get like that?....

After a considerable amount of thinking, it hit me. Of course! That's who! I reached for my reporter's notebook and found the phone number I was looking for and punched those numbers into my cell phone.

It rang a couple of times before I heard, "Hello?"

"Danny. It's Duffy Dixon…."

Chapter Fifty-Five. Charlie

The day had been steady with the normal rushes of people at lunch and dinner. I could not get my mind off Duffy. It seemed crazy to me that this whole mess might be political. The government is like an annoying piece of Velcro: it sticks to everything – even things it shouldn't. I'm not used to dealing with these types of people; I have a feeling things are going to get pretty messy.

As I finished cleaning the last table the door of the restaurant opened. I didn't pay attention to who it was but noticed they kept standing by the hostess stand.

"We're closed," I yelled as I took the rags into the kitchen, still not looking to see who it was. We get drunk stragglers in here all the time. I went to my studio and grabbed a mug I had been saving for just the occasion. I walked back into the restaurant and jumped as I looked up. It was Dr. Payne. "What are you doing here?

"You can call me Derek," he said.

"Well, Derek. It doesn't matter what I call you – we are closed. You can see yourself out." I walked to the door and opened it using my arm to motion that he needed to get the hell out. He just stood there.

"Do your legs not work?" I said.

"I just wanted to see you," he said.

"Well, you see me," I twirled around. "Now leave."

"Come on, Chuck. I was hoping to have a drink with you."

"If you are here for a free drink, you came to the wrong place."

"No, it's not like that at all. I've missed you. Seeing you the other day in the hospital brought back a lot of memories. Have a drink with me, Chuck."

I thought for a moment. I really didn't want to have a drink with him. I have never been the type to catch up with people from my past. If I don't talk to you there's usually a reason. Before I could say anything Derek noticed the mug in my hands and grabbed it.

"Were you coming over to give this to me?"

I nodded my head.

He looked at the mug and read it aloud: "GET THE HELL OUT." He looked up at me as he turned the mug to the back. "AND GIVE THE MUG BACK."

"Yeah, I'm gonna need that mug back," I said.

Derek smiled as he raised the mug above my head so I couldn't get it. "Okay, Miss Charlie. I see how you are going to play this game. I'm holding your mug hostage until you have a drink with me."

He had a charming smile…and my mug. "Fine. But I pick the place and I'm driving separate."

"Okay, then."

I decided to meet him at Lucky 12. I figured it was safe. I got there first and ordered a Corolla Gold while I waited at the bar. I wanted to flag down Jamie but didn't see her. Derek walked in and spotted me immediately. He sat down beside me and ordered a Nags Head IPA. After a few awkward moments Derek finally broke the ice. "What have you been up to for the past, I don't know…"

I interjected. "Since we dated?"

"Well, yeah. Since we dated."

"I've been running Chuck's. Got attacked by a fake shark I named Lester. Now I'm trying to save Chuck's. You?"

"Medical school. I went away for awhile but am back for this fellowship," he said.

"Do you like being a doctor?" I asked.

"I do. Especially when I get to reconnect with people like you." He said as he grabbed my hand. There is no denying that we have quite the history but I don't think I can trust him. I felt my guard go up.

"I'm gonna run to the restroom really quick," I said.

I opened the bathroom door and saw Danny standing by a stall. I went back out and checked the door. There is no way I went in the wrong restroom. The door said: LADIES. "What the hell are you doing in here Danny?"

He looked a little frightened and also completely intoxicated. "Uhhhh…" he muttered. Then I heard a giggle coming from the bathroom stall. Oh no. I walked over to the stall and pushed open the door. It was Jamie. I stood there in disbelief. I looked at Danny. I looked at Jamie.

"The nerve of you two. Danny, you have a wife. Jamie, you have a…uh…Roy. What are you doing?"

Danny just kind of stared at me. I'm not sure he had any thoughts running through his head. Jamie stood up very confidently and then threw up.

"Nice. Very nice you two." I said. "We will talk about this later." I left the bathroom in disgust. I reached into my messenger bag to check my phone. It was blinking. I missed his call. Derek walked up and grabbed my hand. "I found a table for us," he said.

"I need to make a phone call. I'll be right back, okay?" I said.

"Okay. I will be over here'" he said.

I walked outside for a little bit of privacy and fresh air. I dug my phone out and tried to call Bob. Straight to voicemail. "Hey Bob. It's me. I hope you get this message soon. Crap has really hit the fan here. People are talking about a conspiracy and they think your cousin Joe might be in on it. It's getting pretty serious. Call me back as soon as you get this. I miss you."

Chapter Fifty-Six. Danny

I can't believe Chuck caught me and Jam in the bathroom. Just as I was about to get my swerve on. All's we were doin' anyway was celebratin' that extra money I was 'bout to get my hands on. I mean that Dusty feller said that if I'd help him I'd be some sort of hero. I reckon that means I'd be gittin' some sort of money, right?

Anyways, I was here to see if that Joe dude was here. I was supposed to git next to him, hit record on this fancy recordin' machine that Dusty gave me and start talking to him about the pier. See what he might say. Turned out I didn't see no Joe, but Jam, she was there on her day off, and she was lookin' all cute, so we started celebratin'. Damn that Chuck she always butted her nose it where it weren't needed. But one day all of the Outer Banks it be lookin' on ol' Danny a different way when I'm the hero. You just watch and see….

Chapter Fifty-Seven. Bob

Damn! Still playing phone tag with Charlie. All I did was set my phone down on the counter to bring in the last of my suitcases into the house. She only called a couple of minutes ago. Maybe I can still catch her.

"Hello? Bob?" Answered Charlie.

"Yes finally! I was tired of playing phone tag all day." I replied.

"Hold on. I just walked back inside. Too noisy here. Let me go back outside."

"Where are you?" I asked.

"Oh, over at Lucky 12. Long story, I'll fill you in later about it." Charlie responded. A couple of seconds later the background noise quieted down. Charlie was back out in the parking lot I'm guessing.

"Ok. That's better." Charlie said. "Bob, I miss you."

"I miss you too Charlie."

"I'm sorry I flew off the handle at you when you said you were going back to Ohio."

"I'm only back here to land that big account and collect the commission. Plus, whatever I was short of the 50 thousand I was going to take out of my 401k."

"Bob! You can't do that! That's your retirement money!" Charlie chirped into the phone.

"Look Charlie," I began. "If this all works out, then the Tiki Bar can be part of my retirement. Think of it as me investing in your business."

Charlie stopped speaking for a second and let my words sink in. After a few seconds she replied, "Bob, that is so sweet!"

"Charlie, we still have a lot to do and not a lot of time to do it. I'll really be putting in some long hours to close this nursing home account. I want to do it as quickly as I can. Once I do, there will still will be a two week waiting period before I'd collect any money. If we don't want Kirk to lose interest in us being minority partners, we're going to have to get back to him pretty quickly with your money. This is big for us, but we have to remember that it's just small potatoes for him. He could easily become bored with the whole thing and move onto his next project."

"I didn't think about that Bob. Good point. When do you think you'll be back?" Charlie wanted to know.

"I'm really hoping it will be within a month. If so, I think we'll be alright. We'll just keep Kirk informed each step of the way so he knows that we're working towards the 50K."

"Bob?"

"Yes Charlie?"

"Thank you so much for everything. I really don't know where I'd be right now if you and your stupid orthopedic flip-flops didn't show up that day at the Tiki Bar."

"Don't be making fun of the orthopedic flip-flops! They're the very thing that's going to bail us out of this!" I stopped talking, I just heard what I said and even I thought that it was ridiculous. "You know Charlie, I never thought orthopedic flip-flops would one day save the day!"

"Me either Bob. Me either." Charlie giggled into the phone.

"There is one other thing that's been nagging on me though Charlie. That's this notion that you think that good ol' cousin Joe might now be swinging for the other team."

"Yeah. Bob. I can't put my finger on it. He just seems to be sneaking around the perimeter a lot lately."

"Yeah, he called me a couple of times on my drive back to Ohio today. At first I didn't think much of it, but now, I don't know. He's family and all so I don't want to think the worst, but just keep an eye on him please Charlie. I'll try to keep tabs on him best I can from up here too."

"I will. Bob, I can't wait to see you again. And not just because of this whole pier thing and the money. It's more than that. I, well, I just miss you. I'm not a mushy girl, so I hate saying stuff like this, but you get back here as soon as you can."

"I will Charlie. You take care, and I'll check in with you tomorrow."

"Ok Bob, bye."

Both Charlie and I hung up the call. I stood in my living room feeling very lonely all of a sudden. Boris, likely feeling my loneliness, came up and rubbed against me and purred.

Chapter Fifty-Eight. Charlie

With Bob gone, I was left with the task of occupying Kirk and keeping him happy so he doesn't lose interest. Lord knows that isn't going to be easy. The man has had more wives than Kenny Rogers has had facelifts. Lost in thought, I was quickly interrupted. "Charlie," the woman yelled. I got up from my seat and put down the copy of My Outer Banks Home magazine provided by the doctor's office. As I approached the woman who called my name she said, "Hi, my name is Lydia. I am the nurse for Dr. Payne." She walked me back to the room and checked my vitals. When she left the room she said, "Dr. Payne will be right in."

I was sure as shit that Dr. Payne wasn't going to be "right in." What doctor doesn't keep you waiting. Sometimes I think they do it on purpose. I regretted leaving the magazine in the waiting room. 9 hours later there was a knock on the door. Derek walked in.

"Hey, stranger." He said. "I was glad to see your name pop up on the schedule today."

His smile was gorgeous but I had to play it cool. "Well, it was time for my follow up. Like 45 minutes ago."

"Why, yes it was."

He held my hand and wrist carefully in his. I tried not to laugh. His hands were TINY. He was examining the cut and stitches while lightly touching each one. "Things look like they are healing nicely. How have you been feeling?" He asked.

"Not bad. A little sore but nothing crazy."

"Good. Good," he said. "You've been keeping the area clean and dry?"

I immediately thought of the paddleboard expedition that I took the other day. Oops. "Yep, sure have." I tried to sound super confident.

"Good." He said. "I think we need to keep the stitches in a little longer. I would like to see things a little more healed. How about we schedule another follow up for next week to get these taken out?"

Red flags immediately went up. "What about the ukulele contest? I can still do that right? I don't need my wrist stitched for that, do I?"

He was typing something into the computer and immediately stopped. He didn't say anything. Then he started typing again. I started to wonder if he heard me. "Derek?"

He looked up from the computer and walked over to me. "I know this isn't appropriate, but why didn't you come back the other night?"

Crap. I knew he was going to bring this up. I hesitated for a moment and finally found my words. "Derek, we have a lot of history, but we have also just reconnected. I am going through a lot right now."

"I know," he said. "But you can trust me."

"Can I?"

"Of course you can." I could tell he was trying to be reassuring but it honestly came off as trying too hard.

"If I can trust you then answer my question about the ukulele contest."

"Charlie, I don't think it's a good idea. You even said yourself that it was sore."

"But it's fine. It really doesn't bother me."

"Charlie, you asked and I am telling you my professional opinion: don't do it. You're not ready."

That was definitely not the news I was hoping to hear.

He quickly interrupted my self loathing. "How about I stop by the restaurant and pick you up for dinner and a movie?"

"I don't know, Derek."

"You know what? I will swing by, if you want to come then we can go, if not then I will get a drink and we can chat. Either way, I get to see you."

I was unsure about this. You know what they say about guys with tiny hands. You can't trust them.

"Whatever," I said. He walked me out the door and helped me schedule my follow up. As soon as he walked away, I cancelled it.

On my way back home I stopped at the pier outside the restaurant. This little plot of land had been a part of my life since I can remember. I couldn't imagine not waking up to it every morning. I sat there for a minute soaking up every bit of the sun that I could. I rested my hands on the railing of the pier. I had never seen something so beautiful. This is why I loved this place. That and the memories of my dad and I coming to fish here in the summers. They were the best.

A tap on my shoulder pulled me out of my head. I turned around.

"Hey, Chuck. You're just the person I was looking for.

It was Ollie Farkingham.

Chapter Fifty-Nine. Bob

It all seems like another lifetime ago. But here I am driving that same route that I drove to work everyday. Those familiar pangs of dread just gnawing at my stomach as they did each workday morning. Funny, those pains were completely nonexistent when I was on the Outer Banks. But here they are back again. And in full force!

As was my custom I parked in the back lot. All the same cars in all the same parking spots. It was just a sad reminder that nothing ever changes in the corporate world. You give your soul to some faceless entity for what, a check at the end of the week? Although not enough of a check that you have anything left when the next check arrives the following week. And people were happy about this lifestyle? I just simply never got it.

I entered the back door as quietly and as inconspicuously as I could, taking the side hallway to where my desk was located. But, almost like he had been lying in wait since our last phone conversation, there he was. The boss.

"Hey Bob, how's the sausage business?"

I managed a weak smile and a wave as I continued down the hallway to my desk. Really? After all these years he can't update his joke? I can't even imagine how his wife puts up with him. He's got to be the most boring man in the world. It was at this very moment that I realized that my whole disposition on life is severely altered by just being in this building. I'm not normally this much of a SOB.

I got to my desk, flipped on the power switch to my computer. While waiting for it to cycle through and to power on I went to the kitchen for a cup of coffee.

While waiting for the Keurig to spit out the hot, black coffee I felt a huge SMACK on my back. It was Al, one of those "way too happy people" from the front of the building.

"Bob! You're back. Still using a disposable cup I see. When are you going to just break down and bring a cup in from home like the rest of us?"

What I thought was, I won't be in this "factory of sadness" that much longer to have to worry about destroying the environment with my disposable cups. What I said however, was, "yeah Al. I keep forgetting."

I went back to my desk. My computer was on. My first thought was to bring up the webcam on one of my three screens so I can at least feel like I was close to Charlie. Funny, when I sat here last, I had no idea her name was Charlie. I was calling her America at the time. So much has changed for me in the last several weeks. I typed in the web address for the Nags Head webcam. I waited a few seconds for it to come on, and nothing…..The webcam was down. This was not good. All of a sudden this day just became longer for me.

I finished my third sip of my coffee from my disposable cup when, SMACK, on my back. What is it that makes people want to smack me on the back all the time?

"Hey sausage guy!"

It was the boss.

"So, the savior of our orthopedic flip-flop division is back! We sure have missed you. Good thing your vacation is over so you can once again put the ol' nose to the grindstone and sell us some flip-flops. Thankfully we don't have to worry about you going on vacation again for at least another year..."

Is he serious? I thought. He thinks I'm back here for good? Damn, he has no clue I'm only back here long enough to land this nationwide nursing home account so I can collect my commission check and then get the hell out of here! This guy is dumber than a box of rocks. The sooner I land this account the better, for lots of reasons.

I brought up my notes on the nursing home account to refresh my memory and to set up a plan of attack. I must admit however, not being able to see Charlie on the webcam is making it very difficult for me to concentrate.....

Chapter Sixty. Charlie

The sun peeked through the blinds just enough to rouse me from my sleep. It had been a somewhat sleepless night. The kind that kept me looking at the clock and wishing it was morning already. When I finally fell into a restful sleep, morning tapped me on the shoulder as a reminder of the big day ahead. I hope I am ready. I better be ready. I slipped into my flip-flops and headed downstairs for some toast and coffee. I carried my plate to the patio to enjoy the ocean air.

The pier was decently busy with fisherman and on-lookers. I grabbed my ukulele to prep for the first round of tonight's competition at the Front Porch Café. This was as good of a chance as any to get some practice in before the restaurant opened. I strummed a few notes to warm up. My wrist was a little sore but there was no reason not to do the competition. I had been working on a few new songs when I was interrupted.

"Hey, Chuck!"

I looked over to see Duffy Dixon fishing off the pier. He pulled his line out of the water and walked over. I stood up and leaned on the railing; I noticed his fishing rod was missing bait.

"What's going on there?" I pointed at the empty hook.

"Just not my day, I guess," he said.

"It's hard to catch fish without bait. You don't even have a tackle box."

"I'm not really fishing," he said. He was trying to act like he was being super secret.

"No way. I had no idea." I could tell he had no idea I was being sarcastic. He smiled like he was proud of himself.

"I'm trying to catch the scuttlebutt. People gossip. Thought I would try the pier," he said.

"That's not a terrible idea though you might want to reconsider looking like a 1940's newspaper reporter with a fake fishing pole."

He looked a little surprised but shook the comment off. He pointed at my ukulele. "What's going on?"

"Getting ready for the competition," I said.

I could see the wheels turning. "Tell me more."

"There's nothing to tell. I'm trying to win the cash prize to save the restaurant," I said.

The light bulb went off even though it was covered by his hat. "That's perfect," He said as he ran off jotting down notes on an index card. I had no idea what he was planning but that dude is pretty weird. I saw Danny walking up the beach. That was my cue to go inside and get things ready. The mornings always go by quicker than I would like.

By the time I went upstairs and came back down, Danny was starting to set up tables.

"Hey, Danny."

He kind of glared over his shoulder. He turned back around and finished the table he was working on.

"Danny, I don't know what you have going on with Jamie. It's probably none of my business—"

"Damn straight it's none of your business," he snapped back.

"At this point Danny, I don't care. Screw up your life. Screw up your marriage but don't bring it in here. I have enough on my plate right now."

Danny looked a little stunned.

"You know I care about you but I can't deal with all of this. I have the competition tonight. Remember we are closing early for it."

Danny mustered up a "yes, boss" as he looked down at the floor. The day was the same. We didn't speak much. Just the things we had to say. The restaurant stayed busy which helped with some of the awkwardness. I caught myself thinking about Bob and wondered what he was doing. I'd never met anyone like him before.

Before I knew it, it was time to close. Danny and I rushed everyone out, still barely speaking. I went upstairs to get ready for the competition. I changed my clothes and grabbed my ukulele. Danny was still downstairs. "Lock up before you leave," I told him. He waved and said "Break a leg, or whatever you're 'pose to break for good luck, Chuck." It was the first real thing he said to me all day. I smiled. "Thanks, Danny."

I grabbed my bike and headed to the Front Porch Café. I parked my bike and opened the door. The place was packed.

"Hey, Chuck." I heard from across the room. It was Bud. It was good to see a kind face.

"Hey, Bud. Glad to see you."

"I can't wait to see what you have for us tonight."

"Right now it's just butterflies and sweaty palms."

'You'll do great, kiddo." He slapped my back and walked off to clean up a spill. This was all becoming very real. I went back to the seating area for all of the performers. I was nervous. It was finally time. I heard the emcee call my name: "And now for the hometown girl everyone has been dying to see — CHUCK FOSTER."

I took the stage and shook the man's hand. He was a local radio DJ named John Harper. Nice guy but I was so nervous I don't even remember what he looked like. I stepped up to the mic and saw my worst nightmare: Joe, Derek, and off to himself, Duffy Dixon with a cameraman. I had to keep going. It's just like the million open mics at my place.

"Good evening, everyone." I suddenly hated the sound of my own voice. "Tonight I would like to sing you a love song. It's a song about my crush on the Gorton's Fisherman." I could hear the crowd giggle. I could feel my shoulders loosen with their approval.

Fish sticks at the grocery store
Our eyes met at the freezer door
I fell in love right there on the spot
Cause the Gorton's Fisherman makes me hot
I'm preheated, I'm preheated

On his boat the wind blew in my hair
The smell of fish was everywhere
He really wanted to get into my knickers
I said only if you let me wear your big yellow slickers

While we were spooning I whispered in his ear
I really like your ungroomed beard
All of my life where have you been
Gordy you know how to heat up my oven to 350
He uses Pam so it's not sticky

I don't remember saying grace
Woke up in the mornin' tartar sauce was all over the place
And that beer battered goodness all over my face

I don't know if it was the fish or the sauce
The relish or the mayo but it hit the spot
One little taste will leave you in awe
Even Mrs. Paul caught lock jaw

Couldn't resist when he said I wanna get on top of ya
Cause I love the taste of his lemon herb crusted tilapia
I'm preheated

The crowd went nuts as John Harper came back on the stage. "Chuck Foster, everybody!" He shook my hand and patted me on the back. "Our next contestant is Mrs. Paul." The crowd laughed. "Just kidding. Remember folks, the winners of the first round will be announced tomorrow afternoon on 99.1 The Sound so remember to vote."

I got off stage feeling good. I did my best. Now we wait.

Chapter Sixty-One. Danny

'Afore Chuck did that silly Gorton Fisherman song in the contest I met up with that Dusty feller. Or is it Duffy? No matter, that news feller is who I done met up with. Me and him, we got a master plan to get the major news story on these here Outer Banks. We gonna blow everyone outta the water. In fact, Dusty…errr Duffy, whatever, was down at the pier this mornin' collectin' intel. Intel, that's spy talk for information. Least ways, that's what that news feller told me. And I got me a listenin' device taped to my chest. You know the kind they busted that Nixon feller with up there in Washington. Not Washington, North Carolina, you know, the other one. You know like Department of Columbia or somethin'. I just hope when we take this duct tape off me it don't hurt too much. That's what I hope…

Chapter Sixty-Two. George

"Joe!" I shouted into the phone. "Have you been on the 99.1 The Sound website this morning?"

"No George. Any reason I should have been?" Joe asked.

"Seriously Joe? Damn it! I should have teamed myself up with someone with a little competence! Yes Joe! You should have been on the website monitoring the progress of that damn ukulele contest. That bitch girl is way in front! And when I say way in front, I mean no one has a prayer of catching her! That contest is going to bring her something like $20,000. Money she can put right towards her part of that Bashnagel deal!"

There was silence on the other end of the phone.

"Joe dammit! Did you hear what I said?"

"Yeah George. And likely so did everyone else in Dare County. Settle down before you give yourself a coronary."

"Well one of us has to have a fire lit under their ass. Doesn't appear to be you. Of course you also don't have a $5 million dollar deal on the line either."

"George, think about this logically. Even if Charlie wins that $20K, our friend Uncle Sam is going to take half right off the top. She still won't have enough money yet to screw us up. She still has to wait on Bob Evans in Ohio to come through. And that's still going to take up to a month or so. So we're fine. Just settle down a bit, won't ya?"

"I haven't been as successful as I am by being calm Joe. But you wouldn't know about being successful, would you? Glorified dog catcher was all you were until I offered you this finder's fee. And sadly, all you'll ever be is a glorified dog catcher."

Not wanting to continue this conversation any further I hung up the phone without giving Joe a chance to respond.

Chapter Sixty-Three. Joe

I can't believe George. That guy is a real first class ass. Sometimes I think I should screw up this deal just to watch him twist in the wind.....

Chapter Sixty-Four. Charlie

"The votes are in and the people have spoken." John Harper's voice was gold. He was about to announce the winners of the ukulele competition. "The winners of last night's contest are: Regina Phalange, Sandy Butts, Morgan Freeman (not the actor), and last but not least Charlie Foster!"

The whole restaurant went crazy. I could hardly believe it. "Did they just say my name?" Danny had a huge smile on his face. The fight we had was briefly forgotten as he hugged me. "I surely am proud of you, Chuck." He had a grin that only his wife could love. "Thanks, Danny."

I grabbed the microphone "I would say a round of drinks on the house, but I'm trying to save this place!" The restaurant roared and everyone started chanting "Let's save Chuck's! Let's save Chuck's!" It was music to my ears. Then it hit me. I needed to do this all over again in just a few nights. I had some work to do. My thoughts were interrupted by a tap on my shoulder.

"Hey, Chuck."

I was taken back for a moment. "Ollie? I haven't seen you in awhile."

"Good to see you, Chuck. I came here to give you this."

He handed me an envelope. "You've been nominated for an IMA."

"I'm a what?" I asked.

"No, an Indie Movie Award." He said.

"What the Frak? Are you serious?"

He cringed then shook his head yes.

"So this is a thing?" I was suspicious. "Ollie Frakingham-"

"Farkingham." He corrected.

"Whatever. This is real?"

"Yes." He said. I could tell he was getting agitated. "The envelope contains all the details. Congrats." He walked away and sat with a table of people I didn't recognize.

"What was he wantin'?" Danny asked.

"I guess I was nominated for an award or something. For that dumb movie."

Danny looked a little confused but didn't ask any questions. This day was starting to get a little weird. I went into the studio to open the envelope when I heard some footsteps behind me. I turned around to see Duffy Dixon.

"What are you doing here, Duffy?"

"What do you mean? I'm a reporter. I go where there's a story."

"You're in my studio. There's no story here."

"Chuck, you are amazing and you don't even know it. I caught everything on camera. It's magical. The hometown girl caught in a scandal, clawing her way back to victory. I'm gonna break this story. You just wait and see." Duffy winked at me and walked out. I shut the door and finally had a moment of peace. I set the envelope down. That was least of my concern. I took a deep breath and headed for the kitchen door. I could hear two people talking but I couldn't quite make out what they were saying. I was afraid they would see me looking through the window of the door so I ducked below and cracked the door. It was Duffy and Danny. They moved into the pantry and shut the door. I stood up and walked in to see if I could hear anything. It was still muffled. The door swung open. I jumped to the other side of the refrigerator, hoping I wasn't seen. Duffy Dixon walked out. Then Danny walked out. He was itching his chest. "This stuff pulls on my chest pubes, Duff."

Duffy turned around. "It's okay. You'll get used to it."

Danny shook his head unsure if he should believe him. He kept itching his chest. I stepped out from the side of the refrigerator. "Hey Danny, what's going on?"

"Nuthin."

"You seem kind of itchy." I said.

"I think maybe I got into some poison ivy. Reckon I should go to the doctor fer it. I'm gonna need to leave early." He said.

"Okay. So why was Duffy here?"

Danny walked toward the door. "Duffy weren't here. I was on the phone."

I barely caught the last part as he walked out the door.

Chapter Sixty-Five. Ollie Farkingham

I can't believe it. For years I've tried to get an IMA, and just out of the clear blue sky, Boom! Charlie Foster gets nominated. All because she went paddleboarding in rough seas and me and my shark had to save her. That hardly seems fair. I worked my ass off trying to get one. I need to steal the spotlight from her somehow at those awards. It's me that should be recognized. I am the world famous filmmaker after all.

After a few cognacs and some serious thinking, the idea struck like lightening.

Eureka! That's it! I need to get that shark out of the Tiki Bar and into the water again. I looked at the clock on the microwave. I had to really concentrate and squint to see it due to the cognacs. Finally I was able to make out that it was 2 am. But, dammit, this is important.

"Hey Charlie, sorry for the late phone call, but I wanted to congratulate you again on your nomination." I said, trying to hide my slurring from the cognac.

"Uh, thanks Ollie," Charlie said, wiping the sleep from her eyes. "Is that all you wanted?"

"Well, no. I guess not, there is something else."

"Well, what is it Frakingham? I'm trying to sleep!"

"Um, it's Farkingham…."

"Whatever. What do you want?"

"My shark that's in your bar…."

"Yeah."

"Can I have it back? I promise I'll make it up to you."

"If I say yes, can I go back to sleep?" Charlie asked.

"Of course." I replied.

"Great! The shark is all yours. I'm going to back to sleep. Good night Frakingham!"

"It's Farkingham!" I screamed into the phone. It was too late, Charlie had already hung up.

I downed a couple more cognacs and I waited until sun up. I went down the pier with a truck and my special effects guy. He unbolted the shark from its mechanical mounting and we hauled it away. We brought it back to the part of the warehouse I had rented from SPM Landscaping on Kitty Hawk Road and made her seaworthy again.

After a couple of test runs in the sound it was apparent that she ran perfect. Now all I had to do was put my plan into action. I'll get the spotlight away from Charlie. The world may be tuning in to see her win the award, but what they will notice is Ollie Frakingham.....I mean Farkingham. Damn girl.....

Chapter Sixty-Six. Charlie

Ollie came first thing in the morning and hauled away my shark friend, Lester. I was surprised when Frakingham showed up so early; I barely remembered the conversation from the night before. I was sad to see it go. Lester had been an integral part of our restaurant since we bolted it down. He also managed to save my life and scare the piss out of me all at the same time. I am going to miss him.

Finishing up my morning coffee, I headed into the studio to do some painting and make some mugs. I felt stupid for missing Lester. I needed to pull it together. The second round of the competition is tonight. I can't afford to lose this. The painting calmed me but not enough. I grabbed my paddleboard and headed to the ocean. The water was soothing. The ocean always had a way of directing me to what really mattered and today I couldn't stop thinking about Bob. Perhaps that is why I was so sad about Lester.

I looked at my watch. It read 9:45am. I needed to get back inside to get the restaurant ready for opening. I got on my stomach and paddled back in. With the pier to my left, I heard a few people talking about Ollie Frakingham. I looked up and down the shore, there he was and in the water, there was Lester. I pulled my board out of the water and set it against the side of Chuck's. I walked down the beach to Ollie.

"What the hell do you think you're doing, Ollie?"

Ollie jumped. I could tell I startled him. Fishing for words he finally spit out, "Uh, nothing."

"Looks like you're trying to scare the shit out of people again."

"By people do you mean yourself?"

I flipped him off. It's a bad habit of mine.

"Chuck, the shark is mine now."

"Oh yes." I said. "And you owe me big time, remember? We have a contract."

Ollie stood there unsure of what to say.

"Later, Frakingham."

"It's Farkingham," he said.

"Yeah, okay." I walked back to the restaurant. What a morning. Then I had an idea. I grabbed the card off of my desk and dialed the number. It rang, and rang, and rang. Come on, pick up.

"Duffy Dixon." The voice finally answered on the other line.

"Duffy, it's Chuck. You have to get down here now."

"What's going on?"

"It's Frakingham. He has that dumb shark in the water," I said.

"I thought the shark was in your restaurant?"

"Nope. He came and got it this morning. I have no idea what he is up to."

"On my way."

I finished filling the salt and pepper shakers and flipped the "open" sign on the door. I was behind the bar finishing a supplies order when the first customer came in the door.

"Danny, do you mind seating him?"

Danny came bounding out to the front of the restaurant like a little lab puppy with lots of energy. When he finished seating him he came over to the bar. I'm surprised he wasn't panting.

"What's got you so full of energy?" I said.

"Oh, nuttin'. I just thinkin' today is going to be a great day," he said.

I lowered my eyebrows trying to see what in the world was going on in that skull; like most times I didn't see much activity.

"It's a big day, that's for sure." I was pretty sure I was talking to air at this point.

"Whoa! What happened to that shark?" Danny yelled.

"Frakingham picked him up this morning." I said.

Danny had a very puzzled look on his face. I wasn't sure if he was trying to think or if he was holding in a fart.

"He's out there with him right now." I said, pointing outside.

Danny looked out toward the pier.

"I called Duffy. He is out there, too." I said.

"Duffy Dixon? He's here?"

"Yes, Danny."

Danny threw off his apron and ran out the door. I have never seen him run so fast. If he wasn't panting earlier he definitely was now.

"Hey, can someone take my order?"

I totally forgot about that guy. "Yes, sir. Sorry for the wait. Welcome to Chuck's."

Chapter Sixty-Seven. Bob

I dialed the number. I got an answer on the second ring.

"Hello?" Charlie said into her phone.

"Hey Charlie. It's Bob."

"Bob....Bob." Charlie said. "Seems vaguely familiar. Tell me who you are again Bob?" She said, trying not to laugh.

"You know, Bob. The guy who is busting his ass back in Ohio to raise money for your Tiki Bar."

"Oh, now I remember!" Charlie said laughing. "You sell sausage or something equally ridiculous, don't you?"

"Laugh now, but these orthopedic flip-flops may just be the most important thing in our lives at the moment." I said.

"Our lives. He said our lives." Charlie said to herself. He's never referred to anything as ours before.

"Charlie, you still there?"

"Yeah. Sorry Bob, I was just thinking."

"How did the ukulele contest go?"

"Pretty well. I have round 2 coming up tonight." Charlie replied.

"Feel good about it?" I asked.

"I guess so. I really feel like I should win."

"That's great Charlie!"

"How's the nursing home contract. Gonna land that thing finally?"

"Yeah. I sure hope so. I should hear an answer to my proposal any day now. Fingers crossed…..but I do feel comfortable about it."

"That's great Bob!" Charlie exclaimed. "You know, if I haven't already, I want to really thank you for all your help."

"Of course Charlie. I'm glad to do it. Just think, you win tonight and I get confirmation on this deal in the next day or so, then by this time next week, we'll have enough money to give Kirk Bashnagel for your part of the pier."

"I know Bob. It's all pretty exciting and scary…."

Just then the switchboard operator, over the building sound system, said "Call for Bob Evans on line 3. It's the Holy Angels Nursing Home."

"Charlie, I've got to take that. I'll talk to you later?"

"Ok Bob. Miss you!" Charlie said as she hung up her phone.

I hung up my cell phone and hit line 3 on my office phone. "Hi this is Bob Evans."

After listening a few seconds, I placed the phone receiver back on its cradle, totally crestfallen. How do I explain this to Charlie?…..

Chapter Sixty-Eight. Ollie Frakingham, err, Farkingham

"It looks like my mechanical shark is working perfectly," I said to myself. "Time to garner some of that celebrity for myself."

I had put the shark through several practice maneuvers and instructed my mechanic Earl what I wanted done. After I was sure that Earl fully understood, I entered the water. Slowly at first, it was cold! More than I thought it would be. I stood in chest deep water just kind of running in place to try to warm up, but that idiot Earl thought that I was giving him the go ahead sign. He started the shark in my direction. I wasn't ready! Heck, I wasn't even facing the right way. I was facing the shore, my back to the open water, when THUMP! I was hit from behind. Instinctively, I reached back to brush away whatever it was that just hit me, not realizing it was my shark…..

Earl initiated the plan. I wasn't fully prepared to defend myself from its attack like I was supposed to be. I reached down and caught my right hand in the mouth of the steel mechanical shark. The shark instantly jerked left, as was the plan in our fight scene that was being filmed up on the beach. Only I hadn't gotten my hand out of the shark's mouth yet! As the shark jerked, the jagged, steel teeth ripped into my wrist and the force of the shark moving, tore my hand from my wrist! I have never been in such pain before and yelled for Earl to stop!

Earl saw what happened and thought it was all part of the show, so he initiated the next part of our "fight scene." I grabbed the bloody stump on my right hand with my left, trying not to pass out from the pain. My first thought being that I hoped a real shark wouldn't catch the scent of my blood and come swimming in. I didn't have time to think for very long as the mechanical shark came up for it's second staged attack. Trying to protect myself, I reached out with my one still intact hand. No!!!! I screamed.

I heard applause from the gathering people on the beach thinking that this was part of my next movie. "No you idiots!!!!!" I continued to yell. "Earl stop!"

My left hand was now lodged in the shark's mouth. Earl finally realized this may not be a staged act, but rather an accident playing out in the water. Earl moved the shark to my right, away from me, not knowing that my other hand was now in the shark's mouth. With as much ferocity as the first move, my other hand was now ripped from my wrist. I stood in the water with my two bloody stumps at the end of my arms. The pain was so intense the last thing I remembered before passing out was that a real shark had just started to circle me....

Chapter Sixty-Nine. Charlie

"Are you ready for your bill, sir?" I asked.

"Yeah."

"I will be right back with your check."

I finished clearing the plates from his table and walked in the kitchen. Danny came bursting through the back door. He was pale and couldn't put together a sentence. Not that he could put together a great sentence in the first place but this was even worse. I set down the dishes and grabbed his shoulders, trying to calm him down.

"Are you okay, Danny?"

His eyes were wide and he kept stammering.

"Shark....Ollie....nubs..."

"What? You aren't making sense."

Danny pointed out the window. A crowd had gathered; it was hard to see what was happening. "Danny, stay put. I will be right back."

I threw off my apron and ran out the back door. The sun was brutal. It was hard to see through the glare coming off the water. I ran to where the crowd was gathered.

"Now the story is getting interesting," said a voice from behind. I turned around. It was Duffy Dixon.

"It's Ollie," he said. "They called the coast guard."

"Someone needs to help him now," I shouted. No one seemed eager to be going in the water. I really couldn't blame them. By this point he looked about 250 yards off shore. We didn't have a lot of time. I looked around and found a noodle and a boogie board. That was no help. Then I saw a duck mobile parked behind us. Perfect. I ran to the duck mobile. Thelma Lou was written in cursive on the side. "C'mon, Thelma, we have work to do." The keys were still in the ignition. People are too trusting in this town. I felt like I was driving a tanker. I had no idea what to do once I got to Ollie. I just knew I had to get to him. I drove down the beach as I watched the crowd of people part. There was no going back now. I drove in the water and heard all the water boat stuff turn on. I carefully steered my way to Ollie. Thelma Lou seemed to scare off the shark. Now I needed Ollie. I got as close as I could and reached out, "Ollie, grab my hand."

He reached up with two bloody nubs. "What the hell happened to your hands?" I screamed. Ollie started sinking. He lost consciousness. I grabbed a floatation device and jumped in the water. My lifeguard training from high school was coming in handy. Bad choice of words. I grabbed hold of Ollie and got him to Thelma Lou. I was having trouble getting him on the boat when the coast guard came up.

"We can take it from here miss," one of the guys said.

They took Ollie into their boat and back to shore. Two ambulances were waiting. One of the paramedics came up to me, "How are you miss? Are you injured? Do you need anything?"

"I'm feeling a little out of breath. Might need some mouth-to-mouth," I said. The paramedic looked at me blankly. "I'm fine. Just a little shaken up. Thank you." He nodded and returned to the second ambulance.

I looked over and saw the mechanical shark laying on the shore like a beached whale. I walked over and lovingly tapped his fin. "It's time to come back home, Lester, where you are really appreciated."

"Afraid the shark has to come with me."

Startled, I looked over.

"Hi, I'm Lieutenant Dan of the Coast Guard. The shark is part of the investigation."

"Investigation?"

"Yes, Ma'am. This shark has been involved in two attacks, if you will, and we have been here for both of them," he said.

"But the shark isn't real. You know that, right?"

"Yes. But it is evidence. We just want to make sure nothing suspicious is going on, that's all. Two shark attacks with the same radio controlled shark isn't a coincidence."

"True." I had nothing else good to say.

"The only thing I can't figure out is why the first phone call came from Ohio," he said.

"Today?" I asked.

"No. The first so-called shark attack. A guy from Ohio is the one that called it in." His radio started mumbling. "Have to go. Here's my card if you hear or see anything."

I walked up the pier and back to restaurant. I could see Duffy was reporting at the end of the pier but I honestly didn't care. Back in the restaurant, Danny was passed out on the floor and the customer was still sitting at his table.

"Can I have my bill now?" He asked.

"Dude, it's on the house."

It was only 1:30 in the afternoon but I needed a beer. I flipped the open sign to closed, stepped over Danny, and sat in my studio. Could this day get any weirder?

Chapter Seventy. Bob

The news wasn't great from Holy Angels Nursing Home; but it wasn't terrible either. The buyer needed more time before delivery. They have to get measurements from all their residents in all 575 of their facilities across the country, so they can order the proper sized orthopedic flip-flops. I argued that by the time all that was completed; they'd have to start the process over again due to the natural cycles of life, if you catch my drift. Unfortunately my argument fell on deaf ears. They wanted the measurements before ordering. All of this means more time that I have to endure the Boss (the jerk with the sausage jokes, not Bruce Springsteen) and more time being away from Charlie. Not to mention not being able to get the money to her as quickly as we both wanted.

Trying not to stress too much before having to dial Charlie back to let her know the news, I said loudly, "Alexa! Play Carolina in My Mind by James Taylor." The Amazon Echo on my desk came to life…

> In my mind I'm gone to Carolina
> Can't you see the sunshine?
> Can't you just feel the moonshine?
> Ain't it just like a friend of mine
> To hit me from behind?
> Yes, I'm gone to Carolina in my mind

I then reached over to my third computer screen and typed in www.obxwebcams.com and pulled up the Nags Head pier camera. I knew that Danny had it back on line. If I couldn't be there physically, well, at least I could be in my mind......

Wait! What the wha?!?!?!

Is that Charlie coming back to shore behind the wheel of a Duck mobile? Who is that with the Coast Guard? Is that Ollie? And what is all that red paint from?

Just then the camera panned to the right, leaving the scene at the beach. All I saw was the end of the fishing pier, though no one looked liked they were fishing, including that 300 pound shirtless guy with the Daisy Duke shorts, cowboy boots and hat. Seriously, the guy couldn't put on a shirt? Makes watching the webcam hard sometimes. But I digress. Everyone on the pier was paying attention to what was happening on the beach. But what was happening? I couldn't see!

I had to sit at my desk none too patiently as I watched the camera pan several more times, before it was back at the scene on the beach. By then, it appeared whatever happened was already over. The EMTs had Ollie on a stretcher, the sheet covering him stained red, and his wrists, heavily bandaged. So maybe that wasn't paint? Blood, perhaps? I didn't know for sure.

Wait! There was Charlie! I see her! She's talking to that hunky Coast Guard guy. I have to admit, pangs of jealousy hit me pretty hard when I saw that. Now she's looking straight into the camera. Like she's looking straight at me! She's not looking too happy though. Mad in fact. Wonder what that's about....

As Charlie walked back up the beach toward the pier, I got up from my desk and walked into the kitchen to throw my lunch into the microwave. Typically, I go out and grab something, but today I planned on working through lunch so I could get out an hour earlier. When I returned back to my desk with my Hungry Man Turkey Dinner, my cell phone was ringing.....

Without looking to see who it was, I picked it up.

"Hello?"

"Bob.....Charlie. We need to talk...."

Chapter Seventy-One. Charlie

"What is happening? Are you Okay?" Bob asked in a panic.

"Yeah, it's been a little crazy." Then I paused. "Wait, how do you know?"

Bob paused for a moment, "I saw it on the webcam; only the end. What happened? Were you in a duck boat?"

My heart sank. "I think you just confirmed what I wanted to know."

"What do you mean?"

"Why did you come to the Outer Banks in the first place?"

"To get away from my job," he said.

"It had nothing to do with a shark attack you saw on a webcam?" There was silence on the other end of the phone. "You called the coast guard, didn't you?"

"I was trying to help you. I was—"

"Save it, sausage guy. I think I've had all I can take for today." I hung up the phone, Danny was standing behind me. "Glad you woke up from your nap," I said. He had a dumb look on his face. The phone started ringing, it was Bob. I sent it to voicemail.

The restaurant phone rang and Danny answered it, "Yeah, she's right here." He tried to hand the phone to me.

"I'm not here."

"But you're standing right there. It's Bob." He reached the phone out again as if that would make a difference.

"Still not here."

I could hear Danny as I walked toward the studio, still on the phone with Bob. "I don't know what you done Sausage Guy, but she is madder than a wet cat, or whatever is mad when they're wet….."

As I went in the studio door I noticed a red light blinking out of the corner of my eye. I looked up – the webcam. You have got to be kidding me. I am so sick of those things. I ran upstairs and opened the door to my bedroom. I slid open the drawer of my night stand and pulled out my .38 Smith & Wesson Special. It was my Dad's gun. I ran back downstairs and aimed at the first blinking light. Right as I started to pull the trigger, Danny tackled me.

"What the hell ya doin'," he said. The gun flew out of my hand and onto the floor in front of us.

"I'm taking care of the webcams. Something you don't seem to be able to do."

"I'll do it. Just put that golddarn gun away."

I realized that shooting the webcams was probably not the smartest solution but it seemed to be the quickest. Even if I didn't shoot them down, it got Danny's ass moving. When I came back downstairs from putting the gun away, Danny was on a stool working on the first webcam.

"I don't just want them turned off. I want them taken down." I said. "I'm going upstairs to try to get a little rest before the competition."

The Front Porch Café was packed. Duffy Dixon had his usual crew there and Joe and Derek were front row and center. I was going to have to do my best to ignore them. All I know is that I am not going to picture Joe naked. Maybe Derek, though.

John Harper was on stage introducing the other acts. I figured I should get my head out of my butt before he called my name. "Remember," he announced. "The two winners from tonight will compete for the championship on Saturday at the Nags Head pier. The winner gets $20,000 dollars from Ragamuffin Ukuleles and will headline at the Savannah Theatre." The crowd cheered. "With that out of the way let's bring up our first contestant SANDY BUTTS."

I was in a trance for most of the night, trying to get myself into the right headspace. The last person got off stage "Give it up for Morgan Freeman, the girl, not the actor," John announced. "Last but not least we have our hometown girl and hero Charlie Foster. Give it up for Chuck."

The crowd cheered and started chanting "Up Chuck. Up Chuck. Up Chuck." I waved at the crowd, "Thank you," I said. "This song is about my experience selling girl scout cookies."

It started with one free box
Now it's something that we just can't stop
We walk the streets scantily clad
Pedaling cookies for a merit badge

We're selling girl scout cookies, girl scout cookies

We're not in school, no we're playin' hooky
We sell our boxes come take a looky
Give us some cash and you can eat our cookies

Knock, Knock if you don't answer your door
We'll find you at the grocery store
A short little skirt and a low cut sweater
Sell some cookies for a scarlet letter

'Cuz here's the situation:

We've got different prices for different snookie
The more you pay, the better the cookie

Hey baby, you wanna buy some cookies?
They call me daisy-go-round
One taste will turn your world upside down
You know I've been around the block
You can fit twenty cookies in my 8 ounce box
How much for a double dutch? For you $140
I'll give you a snickerdoodle for $60
For an extra $15 your friend can tagalong

'Cuz we're selling girl scout cookies, girl scout cookies
We're not in school, no we're playin' hooky
We sell our boxes come take a looky
Give us some cash and you can eat our cookies

Do-si-dos and lemon cremes
Get tested, you might have something
Ginger snaps and lemonades
Just a few of our street names

But thin mints always sell the best

You can eat chocolate and have fresh breath
But I gotta keep movin', can't keep talkin'
Gotta get my badge for street walkin'

The crowd roared. I could barely hear myself think. Joe looked less than thrilled. I still saw Derek with his clothes off so I have no idea what his face was doing. John came on stage and grabbed the mic, "What a performance from our girl, Chuck. Remember to vote. The winners will be announced tomorrow afternoon on 99.1."

Chapter Seventy-Two. Bob

As I stood in his doorway, and without looking up from his desk, my boss simply said, "Yeah sausage guy, what do you want?"

"Well, sir," I spit the "sir" part out of my mouth, and it had a real bad taste to it. I had no respect for this guy at all. "Well sir," I continued. "I'm not feeling real well. Starting to run a fever I think. I'm going to run home for the rest of the afternoon, and try to feel better, ok?"

"What about the nursing home? What if they call back?"

"They won't be calling back for several days yet. The order is a go, we just have to wait until they collect the sizes for everyone so they know how many of each orthopedic flip-flops to order."

"That sounds a little weird to me sausage guy. You sure this sale is gonna come through?"

"It will come through sir. I'd stake my job on it." I said.

"Sausage guy, that's exactly what you're staking on this sale. If it falls through, so will our orthopedic flip-flop line. And that means we won't need our orthopedic flip-flop salesman anymore. Catch my drift?"

"Yes sir. I'm going to go home now to rest up. Hopefully I'll be back in the morning."

As I turned to leave, the boss yelled out, "Hey sausage guy, don't be stopping off at your restaurant on the way home either…hahahaha!"

"Yeah, good one boss…."

I ran out to my Jeep in the back parking lot, climbed in and raced for home. I had a checklist going in my mind of what I was going to have to do so I didn't forget anything. After about 20 minutes, I got home. I changed into shorts and a t-shirt, grabbed a suitcase and threw a change of clothes in it. Don't figure I'd need more than that. Won't be gone that long, I told myself. I packed my toiletries bag and poured two big bowls of food and two big bowls of water for Boris. Enough to last him until I returned. I cleaned out his litter box and ran back out to my Jeep. I figured that if Miss Charlie Foster won't take any of my calls, well, then, I'm just going to have to drive 10 hours to see her.

I looked at the clock on my dashboard. It showed 10:17 am. If I only stop the one time for gas at the Myersville, Maryland exit on I-70, and at the same time run to the McDonald's next door for coffee, I should get to the Front Porch Cafe by 8:30 tonight. Hopefully the contest will still be going on.

I made really good time on the Pennsylvania Turnpike, got off in Breezewood and headed south on I-70. A short while later I made my planned stop and continued back on my way, only to run into stopped traffic on I-95, south of the Capitol Beltway. Damn! I hadn't figured Washington DC traffic into my calculations. Luckily, the traffic cleared fairly quickly. I was no longer was on pace to arrive by 8:30. It was more like 9:00.

Finally, Fredericksburg, Virginia was in my rear view mirror. I took the bypass around Richmond as I raced south toward Williamsburg and Newport News. I gained a little bit back on the time and finally pulled into the Front Porch at 8:51pm. The lot was full making it hard to find a parking spot. So I pulled around the corner and parked in the Food Lion parking lot.

I got out of my Jeep, ran to the front of the Front Porch and pulled open the glass door. There was Charlie! She was on the makeshift stage that the cafe had put together in front of the far wall. She was playing her heart out. Something about girl scouts being like streetwalkers. Not quite sure what that was about…

Anyway, I digress.

She was up on that stage playing her heart out. The crowd was behind her all the way. Applauding and singing along. Of course, I don't know how anyone else did, since I was driving and missed it; but Charlie was fabulous!

Charlie finished up and John Harper took the stage and reminded everyone to vote. The crowd erupted again. He closed out the show by saying that the two winners will be announced tomorrow afternoon on the 99.1, the Sound.

I walked toward the front of the cafe from my spot in the back of the room to congratulate Charlie. Wait! Is that the doctor from the psychiatric institute? Weird. Wonder why he's there. Wait a minute, why Charlie is talking to him? She seems pretty friendly about it too!

Well, I didn't drive 10 hours to not talk to Charlie, besides, I have to turn right around and go back to Ohio again. I don't have much time, I thought, so I walked up to the both of them.

"Hey Charlie, really good song." I said.

Charlie turned around and looked at me. I don't think she expected me to have shown up like I did.

Chapter Seventy-Three. Charlie

"Bob, what are you doing here?" His clothes were wrinkled, his hair was a mess, and he had bags under his eyes. "Did you get in your car after I hung up?"

Bob nodded in confirmation. "I couldn't leave things the way they were. I needed to see you. I needed to talk to you."

I could feel my heart skip a beat. Bob was a great guy, but with all the crap surrounding the pier, I wasn't sure who I could trust. "Thanks for coming down, Bob. It really does mean a lot."

Derek pushed himself between Bob and I. "Hey, sausage guy. I remember you."

Bob's eyes narrowed and his lips tightened. I have seen that look before. I hadn't known Bob long but I knew what it meant. Showtime.

"Hey, aren't you the guy that helped lock Charlie up in the psych ward?"

Derek took a step back. "That's right," Bob said. "Keep on steppin'."

"I was just trying to help her."

"Yeah, help her lose the restaurant," Bob said. "You knew she wasn't suicidal."

Derek clenched his fists and took a step forward. As much as I was enjoying two men arguing over me, I knew this wasn't going to end well. "Hey. Break it up before I neuter you both," I yelled. I grabbed each of them by their ears and dragged them outside to the parking lot. "Are you two nuts?"

Bob and Derek looked like two children getting in trouble. They were each rubbing their earlobes. I would have laughed if I wouldn't have given up my position of power. "I am not doing this tonight," I continued. "Honestly, you both suck. Derek, you are a terrible doctor. I thought you might be in on this whole thing but I am starting to think that maybe you just suck. Go back to school and start thinking with the right head. Or better yet, be an underwear model. Trust me, from what I saw tonight, you have the body to do it." Derek raised his eyebrow. "Don't ask," I said.

Derek started to say something but I cut him off. "Shut up and let me speak. Bob. I like you. I even thought I might be falling for you but what the hell is going on with the webcams and Ohio? For awhile you were one of the only people I trusted but now…I honestly don't know."

They were both staring at their feet. Finally, Derek looked up. "I'm gonna head out now." I nodded at him in approval. I refused to give him anything more. Boys are dumb. Derek got in his car and drove away. Watching the sad walk back to his car provided a solid two minutes of awkward silence between Bob and I.

"Bob. Let's call a timeout on this thing. You did just drive from Ohio to see me. Wanna grab a drink at Lucky 12?"

Bob's eyes perked up.

"But this doesn't mean anything. I'm just thirsty."

"Yes, ma'am." Bob grabbed my bike and threw it in the back of his Jeep. He opened up the passenger door like a gentleman. As I buckled my seat belt I could see his face partially lit by the moon. I had a hard time believing that I couldn't trust him. I've never had someone drive all day just because I wouldn't pick up the phone. I held onto his arm and rested my head on his shoulder. I didn't have to figure this out tonight.

Bob poked me in the side, trying to keep a straight face. "So you don't think I would make a good underwear model?"

Chapter Seventy-Four. Ollie Farkingham

Looking at my chart, the doctor came into my room at the Outer Banks Hospital. "Mr Frakingham…" he said.

"That's Farkingham doc." I replied.

"Oh, right. Sorry. Well, we were not able to recover your hands from the shark's mouth. I'm afraid the best we could do is to set you up with artificial hands."

I laid back in my bed, looking at the bandages where my hands used to be. Then an idea hit me. "Hey doc, can I have a hook for my left hand?"

"You mean like Captain Hook?" The doctor asked.

"Exactly like Captain Hook!" I exclaimed. Thinking to myself about all the publicity I would get for this latest film. I can see it now, I said to the doctor, "World Famous Filmmaker Ollie Farkingham vs. The Great White!"

"But Mr Frakingham…"

"God Damn it! It's Farkingham!" I shouted.

"Yeah, right. Sorry again." The doctor said. "But it wasn't a great white that got you. It was a bull shark."

"And that, my good man, is why you are a doctor and I am a world renown filmmaker. A bull shark doesn't sell as well as a great white. Just leave the movie making to me."

"Ok Mr Frakingham. I'll just leave you alone now and set up the hook for your left hand." The doctor said as he left my room.

"It's Farkingham…." I said under my breath. Oh, never mind, I thought, as the pain medication took hold and I drifted back to sl…..zzzzzzz.

Chapter Seventy-Five. Kirk Bashnagel

"Hi, Charlie. Kirk here." I said into the phone.

"Oh, hey Kirk. Sorry it is so loud, I'm at the Lucky 12 with Bob right now. Let me step outside where I can hear you better."

A few moments later the noise dissipated as Charlie walked outside to the parking lot.

"Hey Kirk. That's better. I can hear you now. What's up?"

"Just haven't touched base with you in a little while. I wanted to make sure you were still on this pier thing. I don't usually wait this long on a project."

"Yes, for sure." Charlie said to me. "I am so sorry that it is taking this long. I'm just trying to raise the funds right now."

"Any idea how much longer I need to put this project on hold? To be honest, I want to put this in my rear view mirror and move on to other things."

"I know." Charlie said. "I should have close to half of it in the next few days, if all goes according to plan."

"The ukulele contest?" I asked.

"Yes sir."

"That's kinda iffy, isn't it Charlie?" I asked.

"I don't think so sir. I am pretty confident that I will have this thing in the bag." Charlie replied.

"Ok. If you do have it in the bag, what about the other half?"

"Well Kirk, that date is still up in the air a bit. My friend Bob Evans just sold a nursing home a new order of orthopedic flip-flops. His commission check will cover the other half. We're just not sure yet when exactly he'll get that check. We're hoping in the next three weeks or so."

"So, let me get this straight," I said. "Your part of this investment is coming from a ukulele contest and orthopedic flip-flops?"

"It does kind of sound wacky when you say it out loud I guess." Charlie said.

"Uh, yeah. Well I will say, this is the weirdest deal I've ever been a part of. But, I'll be honest, I'm not sure I can hold out another three weeks on this." I told Charlie.

There was silence on the other end of the phone for what seemed like a minute or two. Finally Charlie said, "I'll tell you what Kirk. If I don't win this contest, I'm out of the running, regardless how long it would take Bob to get his commission check. So how about this, if I do win, and I do get my prize money, how about I turn that over to you as a down payment. If Bob doesn't come through in three weeks with his end, you keep my prize money, no questions asked. Would you be willing to wait then?"

I had to admit, it did sound interesting to me. It wouldn't cost me anything really to wait those three weeks. And if at the end of it, if there is no deal in place, I get to pocket 20 G's. "Ok, Charlie," I said. "You have a deal. Bring me the money if you win and I'll wait three more weeks. But if you don't win the contest, then I move on and the deal is off."

I could hear Charlie gulp loudly before answering. "Yes Kirk. That's the deal. We have an agreement."

Chapter Seventy-Six. Charlie

I walked into Lucky 12 with a lump in my throat. Bob was sitting at the bar where I had left him. I couldn't help but wonder if I just made a really stupid mistake.

I sat down on the barstool beside Bob. He put his hand on my knee, "Everything okay?" He asked.

"I need a shot…something really strong." I was talking to no one in particular but was hoping for a shot glass to magically appear in front of me.

The bartender looked our way. Bob pointed at me, "You heard the lady."

A shot glass appeared.

"Now tell me what is going on, Chuck."

I took a deep breath, downed the shot, and felt it burn all the way down. I felt warm, fuzzy, and numb enough to tell the truth. I told Bob about Kirk as fast as I could. Bob stared at me. "You did what?"

"Yeah," I said. "I bet the competition money. If I lose then I lose everything."

Bob's face softened as he reached for both of my hands. "You bought us some time," he said. "We won't lose."

I buried myself into his chest and felt safe and familiar. "Can I ask you something?"

"Of course," Bob said.

"What happened with the 9-1-1 call?"

Bob sighed and took a seat. I wasn't sure I wanted to know the answer but I also knew that I needed to know the answer.

"So?" I said. "Were you the one that called?"

"Yes," he said. "But hear me out."

I nodded for him to continue. "I'm listening."

"I used to watch the Nags Head pier webcams as a way to escape work. Then I saw you one day. And then I liked seeing you. I never dreamed we would ever meet."

"So how did the phone call happen?" I asked.

"I saw the shark attack and I felt helpless. The only thing I could think about was calling the coast guard. I didn't know you but I knew I didn't want to lose you."

"So it had nothing to do with Joe?"

"Joe? No. Not at all," he said.

I felt a sense of relief. I knew I was over thinking things. I grabbed his hand, "It's still a little creepy."

Bob managed a laugh. "It's been a long day," he said.

"I know. Want to crash at my place for a quick nap before heading back?"

"Sure." Bob answered.

We walked to Bob's jeep in the Lucky 12 parking lot. He opened the door and Joe jumped out. Bob immediately stepped in front of me.

"What are you doing here, Joe?"

"I drove by and saw your jeep. Get in." Joe said.

"Get in to my own car?" asked Bob.

Joe pulled a gun from his waistband and pointed it at both of us. He tied our hands together and shoved us into the back seat. This guy has some serious issues.

"I talked to Kirk earlier. I'm trying to push this deal through and you keep getting in the way. I'm going to see to it that we don't need to worry about either of you. This deal is going to make me rich. I can finally get out of this hell hole."

"Joe, this doesn't make any sense. Just stop," said Bob.

"Oh no. You aren't going to outshine me this time, cuz. I will take care of you both."

This was not how I saw things going. Joe kept driving. I could see the water out the right window. I had no idea where he was going but I knew it wasn't going to be good and I knew we needed a plan.

Chapter Seventy-Seven. Danny

What the hell? I was at Lucky 12 tonight trying to see my sweet Jam, but her car weren't there. But know what? I saw somethin' I didn't expect to see. No siree….Why was that Joe feller stickin' a gun into the ribs of his own kin? That didn't seem right. Then I seen him force both the sausage guy and Charlie into that Jeep. I seen them drive away too. Seemed to me they was heading back towards Roanoke Island.

I reached for my cell phone. He answered on the second ring….

"Hello?"

"Yo Dusty…"

"It's Duff……Oh, never mind. What do you want Danny?"

"Hey. Just saw somethin' I don't think I was 'spose to see."

"What's that?" Duffy asked.

"That dog catcher feller just threw his cousin, the sausage guy, and Charlie into a Jeep. He had a gun, tied their hands nice and good and drove away."

 Duffy didn't say anything right away, so I said, "You still there Dusty?"

"Yeah, I'm still here. You sure about what you saw? Absolutely sure?" Duffy asked.

"Yeah, my eyes, they work just fine Dusty."

"You weren't drinking, were you Danny?"

"Nah, sir. I mean I was gonna, but Jam wasn't there, so I didn't go in."

"Ok." Duffy said. "Which way did they go?"

"Well, they be headin' down the beach road from Lucky 12 headin' south.

"Danny, do you have a car?" Duffy asked.

"Nah, I had to hitchhike here. I was hopin' that Jam was gonna drive me back home."

"Can you get a car?"

"I reckon I can, if I git home. My wife has hers there."

"Ok, try and git, I mean, get a car. I'll be back in touch. I have some calls to make."

Chapter Seventy-Eight. Duffy Dixon

I hung up my cell phone with that idiot Danny and sat back in my chair reflecting on everything happening. I thought of the time I surprised both Joe and George as they were "innocently" having coffee at the Morning View. Has to be something there, I thought. I was always at my best when I play my hunches, and right now the hair is standing up on the back of my neck. I immediately made some phone calls. I knew for a fact that my network of people will help tell me what I needed to know right now.

After 12 to 15 calls, I found what I was looking for. George was in the bar at JK's having a drink. I got in my car and made my way down the bypass to play out my hunch.

"Hey George," I said as I walked into the bar at JK's.

"Whadda you want you nosey little SOB?" George snapped back.

"Ah, just as pleasant as always," I replied. "But I think you should be nicer to the guy who is very soon to be your business partner."

"What are you yammering about Dixon?"

"Well, George, you said it yourself the other day. You said I work for a crap station. I got to thinking about that and decided that you were right. I do work for a crap station and I figured I should do something to get out."

"What's that got to do with me and you being business partners?" George asked.

"George, it's got everything to do with it."

"Go away and leave me alone. I'd prefer to drink in peace." George snapped.

"Ok, George, but before I do, I figured that you might want to know that Joe has already launched your plan into action."

"Joe? I don't know any Joe. You're talking out your ass again Dixon." George growled.

"Oh yes you do George. Remember, you and Joe had coffee together at Morning View a little while back. I came in and said hi to you both?"

"Oh yeah, that Joe." George replied. "Forgot about him. He's a nobody. But I don't know nothin' about no plan being launched."

"Oh sure you do George." I said. "Just a few minutes ago Joe grabbed that Bob guy from Ohio and Charlie Foster at gunpoint and drove away into the night."

The color drained instantly from George's perfectly tanned face. He looked as white as those ghost crabs that scurry along the beach at night.

Just then, the bartender came up and asked George if he'd like another Crown on the rocks.

"No thanks." George stammered. "I have to go."

Smiling that my hunch seemed to have paid off handsomely, I told the bartender that I would like a Pinot Noir.

Chapter Seventy-Nine. Charlie

Somehow the night managed to get darker. I had no idea where we were headed. I could tell Joe was texting with someone. I elbowed Bob and gestured toward Joe, hoping he could see who he was texting. Neither of us could see much of anything.

"Hey, what's all that commotion back there?" Barked Joe.

Bob finally spoke. "Joe this is ridiculous, man. Turn the car around and let's go home. We can figure this out in the morning."

Joe slammed on the brakes and pulled over to the side of the road. He pointed the gun at Bob. "Shut up or I'll end it for both of you. You are not going to ruin things for me, again."

Tough talk for a guy in orthopedic flip-flops.

Joe got back on the road and started texting again. A little while later a car approached from behind. It was the first sign of anyone since we were abducted from the Lucky 12 parking lot. I knew I had to make the most of the situation. I slid my hands underneath me and back in front, like a reverse jump rope. As I was devising a plan to loosen the rope around my wrists, the car drove wildly around us and Joe sped up to keep him in our sights. We went from total darkness to a residential area. The guy was driving like a mad man. He blew through a stop sign and almost side swiped a car. Forget about the gun, I was starting to think we might not survive Joe's driving.

We stopped in a dimly lit driveway in front of a house. The guy Joe followed got out of his car first and gave a hand signal. Then Joe got out of the car. The guy from the other car came to my door and Joe went to Bob's side. They opened the doors and grabbed each of us by the neck. I could feel the gun in the small of my back. They walked us up to the front door. A pack of cats scattered when he opened it. The lighting made the inside look yellow and dirty. But then again, maybe it wasn't the lighting. They forced us over to a tweed couch. The guy bent down in front of me.

"Where are my manners?" He said. "My name is Poolside Tommy."

"Okay." I said.

"That wasn't an invitation to talk." He snapped back.

Bob and I looked at each other, unsure of what to do, and unsure of what we were smelling. It was a mixture of cat pee, mold, dirty fish and reptile tanks. They were everywhere. Joe stood by the front door with his gun. They have either done this before or Joe was shitting his pants. It was hard to tell. Joe always kind of looked like he was about to poop himself.

"It seems you two have been causing us a little bit trouble." Said Poolside Tommy.

"How is that?" Asked Bob.

"This pier business is getting in the way of my plans. This goes deeper than you think." He said.

"How is saving my restaurant affecting you or that douche bag over there?"

"That ain't none of your business sweetheart. What is your business is that you two have exclusive invitations to a pool party. I throw the best pool parties." He almost snarled when he said it. Poolside Tommy's phone started ringing, "My milkshake brings all the boys to the yard." He pulled it out of his pocket and looked at Joe. "Watch them."

I was confused by his choice of ringtone but felt it was not a great time to bring it up.

He walked into another room. He sounded annoyed but I couldn't understand what he was saying. When he walked back in he looked even more pissed than before. "Alright you two. It's time to get you ready for this pool party. Did I mention I throw the best pool parties?"

"Yep." We said together under our breaths.

I didn't know how we were going to get ourselves out of this. There was no way I was going down like this. I would die if I didn't try and I would die if I did. I would much rather die trying.

Joe and Poolside Tommy grabbed us by our necks and had the guns in our backs. I could see the pool through the sliding glass doors. The doors were dirty and foggy. I saw something moving around in the pool. We went through the doors to a dirty, green, in-ground pool. It looked to be about 20 years past its heyday. There were two alligators in the pool.

"I want you guys to meet Mork and Mindy. They are expecting you for dinner," said Poolside Tommy.

I am not getting eaten by an alligator. This isn't happening right now. They took us to the edge of the pool. When a gun shot went off in the air.

"You let them two fellers go."

I looked over my shoulder to see Danny with my gun. He shot it in the air again. "Let them go."

Chapter Eighty. Bob

As soon as I heard the gunfire break out, I dove on top of
Charlie to shield her from it. Our hands were still tied, but
we were able to roll into the darkness of the bushes below.
I only wished those sand spurs weren't there…

From under the bushes I heard Danny yell out: "Drop your
gun dog catcher!"

Joe took a minute to survey the current situation. With
Danny holding his gun against Joe's back, Joe didn't see
any alternative but to drop his.

As Danny held cousin Joe and Poolside Tommy at bay
with Charlie's gun, Charlie, with her hands still in front of
her had managed to untie me. I then did the same for her.
We both stood, and for a second we pulled sand spurs out
of our arms and legs. Danny stood there waving that gun
back and forth from Joe, and then back to Poolside
Tommy. I'll be honest, I, myself, didn't trust Danny with
that gun. Hell that boy could just as easily shoot me and
Charlie, and even himself, as much as he was likely to
shoot the bad guys.

As I turned my attention from the sand spurs to the figures
standing in the darkness, I noticed Poolside Tommy
inching closer and closer to the gun that he had dropped on
the ground. I sprung forward and pounced on it before
Tommy had a chance. Great….more sand spurs, I thought.
Quickly I jumped to my feet, ignoring the needles of the
spurs, and helped Danny cover both Tommy and Joe.

"Hey Danny! How did you find us?" Charlie yelled out.

"Well, Chuck," Danny said. "That news feller, Dusty. Well, he put a tracker on the sausage guy's Jeep. Put one on yours too. He knowed sooner or later knowing where you two was would come in handy."

"Never in my life have I ever been so happy to have my rights violated," Charlie laughed.

Figuring we needed to do something to further gain the upper hand I shouted to Charlie: "Grab the rope and tie these two up real nice and tight like!"

"You got it." Charlie replied.

"In fact tie them face-to-face to that cypress tree over there." I further instructed.

Charlie went to work with the ropes, and after both Joe and Poolside Tommy were secured to the cypress, I checked the knots to make sure they were nice and secure. They were. Just then Joe's cell phone rang. I pulled it from the back pocket of his jeans and looked at it. According to the caller ID it was George.

With the gun firmly planted in his back I said to Joe, "Ok cuz. You're gonna answer this call and you're gonna be nice and calm about it too. No funny stuff" I then poked the gun deeper into his back to show him I meant business.

I turned the cell phone's speaker on and nodded my head to indicate to Joe to start talking.

"Hello?" Joe said.

From the cell phone speaker George yelled out: "Joe you damned fool! What are you doing? I told you not to make any moves without me!"

"Um, what are you talking about George?" Joe stammered into the phone.

"Don't play dumb with me Joe!" George snarled. "That damn pesky TV reporter said you took the sausage guy and that bitch from the pier hostage!"

"Why would I do that George?" Joe replied.

"Because you're that damned stupid. That's why! I knew I should have never gotten into bed with you on this." George yelled. "I want you at my house in the next half hour! Do you understand me? A half hour!"

With that George hung up his side of the call.

"So now what smart guy?" Joe asked me with as much venom in his voice as he could muster.

"Let me think a second," I said.

I turned my attention to the alligators in the pool for a second. I wanted to make sure we were still out of their reach. Being on the outside of the pool fence, we were at the moment. I paced the yard and after a few seconds I turned back to Joe.

"Where does George live?" I asked.

"You think I'm gonna tell you that? You can go to hell!" Joe spit out.

Thinking for another second, I told Danny to sit on Poolside Tommy and ol' cousin Joe. "Call the police and wait here for either me to come back, or the sheriff to get here. And don't let them get away for God sakes!"

"Come on Charlie! You're coming with me."

I got behind the wheel of my Jeep as Charlie jumped into the shotgun seat. I put the Jeep into gear. Dirt and gravel from my wheels spit out behind me as I peeled out of the driveway. Once I got out onto the street I reached for my cell phone, dialed a number, and waited for an answer......

"Hello, Duffy? It's me Bob....."

Chapter Eighty-One. Charlie

Bob took the phone from his ear and looked at the screen. "Duffy either hung up on me or I dropped his call."

"Call back," I said.

Bob dialed the number and this time left it on speaker phone. It went directly to Duffy's voicemail. "That's weird," Bob said.

"Incredibly," I said. I looked up to see headlights coming right at us. "Bob, watch out."

Bob jerked the wheel to miss the car. The car hit the front driver's side door and spun us into the ditch. "Bob, are you okay?"

"Yeah, I think so." There was blood on his shirt.

"Bob, you're bleeding."

"I can see that." Even in pain he couldn't resist being sarcastic. "I can't open my door," he said.

I tried my door. I had to give it a good shove but I was able to slip out. I yanked on it from the outside handle and was able to open it a little more. I climbed back in and unbuckled Bob's seatbelt. "Come out this way," I said.

As Bob was gingerly getting out of the car I felt sweat drip down my face. I wiped it away to see blood covering my hand. "Oh, Charlie." Bob said. "You have a bad cut above your eye."

"I can see that." I said as I went around to the back of the Jeep. I found a bag and grabbed a t-shirt and an orthopedic flip-flop. "What are you doing with that?" Asked Bob. "That was the overnight bag I packed."

"I'm splinting your arm." I said. I made a sling out of the t-shirt and splinted his forearm with the flip-flop. "I hate to admit it but these dumb flips-flops have been useful." We both mustered a laugh. I grabbed the second shirt and tied it around my head to soak up some of the blood and cover the gash above my eye. I heard a noise. "What was that?"

"What was what?" Asked Bob.

I heard it again. "That."

It sounded like someone moaning. Bob and I walked around the Jeep to find the car that hit us, flipped on its top down in a ditch along the side of the road. I looked in the driver's side window. "Are you okay?" I asked. The driver moaned again. I looked back at Bob, "What should I do?"

"Can you see who it is?"

"Not really." I went to the other side of the car. "Are you okay?"
The driver moaned and moved their head a little. "Oh my gosh." I gasped. "It's Duffy."

"Really?" Asked Bob.

"No, It's Gene Autry. Yes, It's Duffy."

Bob searched for his phone but couldn't find it. We heard sirens in the background, no doubt going to Poolside Tommy's. "My bike is still in the back of the Jeep. I will go back to Poolside Tommy's and try to catch the police there."

"I don't want you going there by yourself," said Bob.

"What other choice do we have. I don't know where the hell we are. I won't go in until I know the police are there."

"Promise me you will wait for the police. And don't go in the house. Period."

"I promise. We aren't that far away, after all."

I grabbed my bike out of the back of the Jeep. My head was pounding and I was feeling a little lightheaded but I knew I needed to power through to get some help. I gave Bob a hug. "I will be back shortly."

I started down the road to Poolside Tommy's. I wasn't sure if it was blood or sweat dripping down my face but I knew I had to find the police. I saw the lights ahead pulling into the driveway. I tried to speed up my pedaling to catch at least one of them before they went in the house. My bike hit some loose gravel and I lost control. I flipped over the handle bars and landed in the driveway beside a police car. I tried to muster the strength to get up, but was having trouble. Someone walked over and bent down to take a look at me. Things got really hazy and then black...

Chapter Eighty-Two. Bob

Charlie has been gone a good long while now. A half hour? Maybe an hour? I wasn't sure. Duffy still laid in his car drifting in and out of consciousness. No doubt we couldn't stay out here much longer. I still couldn't find my phone, but as I tried to free Duffy from his seatbelt, I found his. I dialed 911.

"911. What is your emergency?"

"Hi, my name is Bob Evans." I said into the phone. "I've been involved in a car crash."

"What is your location Mr Evans?"

"Um, I'm not really sure. I was kidnapped by my cousin and some guy named Poolside Tommy. We're near Poolside Tommy's house. Ever heard of him?"

"No sir. Can you tell me the general area in which you're in?"

I heard Duffy groan something. I pulled myself closer to hear what he had to say. Though I'll admit, that wasn't an easy thing to do with just the one good arm. I leaned in, but couldn't make out it out….

"Sir?" The 911 operator said. "Is there someone with you? Are there any injuries?"

Turning my attention back to the phone, I replied: "Yes. Duffy Dixon from ABC TV is here. He's hurt. I have a lacerated arm and Charlie Foster was here too. She was also hurt. A cut on her head. But she left looking for help. She heard sirens and went back to see if she could direct help back to us. But she's been gone a while now. Can you see what other dispatches may have been made in the last hour to hour and a half?"

"Looking now sir. Stay with me." The 911 operator instructed.

I heard Duffy groan out the same word again. I leaned in even closer for a better position to hear what he was saying. "Esfake" is what I heard.

"Say that again Duffy!" I pleaded.

"Esfake….Esfake." Duffy spit out again.

"Sir, you still there?" The 911 operator asked.

"Yes operator. I'm still here."

"Sir. I see that we have dispatched out of Dare County to four different locations in the last couple hours. Can you at least narrow down which part of the county you're in?"

"No operator! I was blindfolded from the time I was taken at gun point."

From the background I heard Duffy again say out loud "Esfake!"

"Is that the other person I heard?" The 911 operator asked.

"Yes. That's Duffy Dixon."

"What is that he said sir?"

"I don't know operator. It sounds he's saying Esfake."

After a momentary pause, the 911 operator asked, "Could he be saying East Lake?"

"He might be. I don't know for sure. Why?"

"We had a call for East Lake almost an hour ago. I'll send one of those squads back down the road to look for you."

"Thank you operator. We're in a ditch, so I'll keep an eye out for him."

"Yes sir. Stay on the line with me while you wait."

"I will. Thank you."

I switched the phone over to speaker mode and set it down while I positioned myself on the side of the road with my one good arm. It wasn't more than two or three minutes before I saw a police cruiser slowly heading down the road with its floodlight sweeping from side to side looking for us. "I see the police car!" I yelled into the phone's receiver.

I waved with my one good arm as the car made its way down the road closer to where I was at the side of the ditch. I was still waving, but the driver still hadn't seen me. So I yelled out, "Hey! Over here!"

That seemed to have attracted the attention of the driver in the squad car as he directed the spotlight in my general direction. As he pointed the spotlight off to my right I saw the driver lit up in the ambient light of that searchlight. "Wait! It couldn't be…..NO!"

"911 Operator! Send out a different dispatch. The driver of this police car is Poolside Tommy……"

Chapter Eighty-Three. Charlie

I woke up in the back of a car. My head was pounding and, evidently from the blood on the seat, still bleeding. A man was driving the car. I could only see the back of his head and could hear him mumbling something. It was dark and hard to see through the bars separating the front of the police cruiser from the back. I felt my heart relax a little as the realization came that I was in the back of a police cruiser. The man in the front seat must be an officer. I felt a wave of relief go through my body. I was safe.

It was at that point that I heard a call come in from the dispatcher about an accident in East Lake. I could only wonder if that was Bob they were talking about. I heard the man driving the car say "Copy that, I'm on my way."

The voice sounded oddly familiar. I rolled over to my left side trying to push myself up to see the driver when we hit a pothole that jolted me back onto the seat. My entire left side screamed in pain. I was quickly reminded that I had flown off my bike by the cop car.

A cell phone rang. It was "My milkshake brings all the boys to the yard." It was all I could do to hold back laughter until my brain kicked in — POOLSIDE TOMMY. It couldn't be. No way.

He answered the phone. "Yeah, I'm on my way now. I got the girl in the back. She's dead. I'm on my way to finish off the other guy." Then he hung up the phone. It was definitely him.

He thinks I'm dead. Why would he think I am dead? Didn't matter. I needed to play dead and figure out a plan. I laid across the seat and looked up at the stars through the window. If it wasn't for my life being at stake, this really was turning out to be a beautiful night.

The car slowed down. He turned the flood light on. It went back and forth several times. "Here kitty, kitty, kitty." He kept saying over and over. I could feel a chill run down my spine. I could only hope that we were on the wrong road or that Bob somehow got away from there.

Then I heard Bob. "Hey! Over here!"

Oh no.

Poolside Tommy giggled to himself. "Gotcha."

I hadn't thought of a plan yet. How was I going to stop this guy? He slammed on his brakes and got out of the car. Bob looked like a deer caught in headlights.

"You thought you could run from me?"

"Where's Charlie?" Asked Bob.

It was all I could do not to tell him I was here and okay. Minus the blood. And the concussion.

"Who? Oh, the girl? She's dead."

Poolside Tommy stepped in front of the police car blocking my view. I tried to move but still couldn't see much until Poolside Tommy hit the hood of the car. Was that Bob? Holy cow that was Bob. He's a regular Jim Abbott, that guy.

They slid off the hood. Poolside Tommy was standing over Bob with a gun drawn. Then I heard a shot. What happened? Forgetting I was supposed to be dead I sprang up looking for Bob. Poolside Tommy was facedown on the ground. Bob stood up looking around. I still wasn't sure what happened. I knocked on the window trying to get his attention. He finally looked up and came over to the car.

"Charlie?''

He opened the door and I fell into his arm. Yes, his arm. We didn't say much of anything, both of us just glad the other was still alive.

I finally broke the silence. "Hey, Bob. What happened to Poolside Tommy?"

Chapter Eighty-Four. Bob

"He messed with the wrong guy, is what happened to Poolside Tommy," I said proudly holding onto Charlie with my one good wing. "He ought not have told me you were dead. I figured I had nothing to lose at that point."

"Oh Bob, you're my hero!" Charlie swooned.

Ok. She didn't really say that. But it would have been damn cool if she had. What she really said was something like, "Let's get the hell out of here!"

Figuring that was a fairly good idea, Charlie and I jumped into the squad car. She in the passenger seat; me on the driver side. With the one good arm I had, I threw the car into drive and then grabbed hold of the wheel as I raced back toward Poolside Tommy's house. "Let's go find the other cops," I said to Charlie.

Rather than answering me back, Charlie just gave me a dazed look, and I knew that I was going to have to get her medical attention soon. Not to mention getting some for Duffy Dixon, who was still laying out there in the ditch.

Tommy's house, thankfully, wasn't quite a mile away, so I was able to get us there pretty quickly. But I'll be honest, I was not expecting to find what I found.

I had figured that Poolside Tommy merely slipped away from the cops and stole one of their vehicles. However, what Charlie and I found at the house told us a completely different story.

To the cypress tree to the right of where we had tied both Tommy and cousin Joe, we found four Dare County deputies secured with their own handcuffs. They were all unconscious. Apparently Joe and Tommy had managed to get the drop on them somehow. Maybe Tommy and Joe were able to free themselves before the cops got there. Perhaps it was after the cops untied them. Maybe they jumped the deputies then. I wasn't sure, and at this point, it didn't matter. As I reached into the deputies' pockets to try to find the keys to their own handcuffs, I heard Charlie yell out, "Bob! Over here! Quick! You're not gonna believe this!"

I went running over to Charlie, who was at the edge of the fence surrounding the pool where the alligators were kept. In the pool floating face down was my cousin Joe. Various chunks of his body missing, apparently caused by the gators.

At first I didn't say anything. I just looked at Joe's lifeless body in the pool, the alligators swimming around him. Finally, I said, "That's it. We need to call for some help here. Don't touch anything."

I ran back to the squad car and grabbed the radio receiver. "Hello?" I said into it. "Hello? This is Bob Evans. Someone please answer."

A second later came a reply. It sounded like the same 911 operator that took my initial call. "This is dispatch. Go ahead," the voice said.

"Hi. This is Bob Evans," I replied. "I made a call into 911 a bit ago about a car wreck in East Lake."

"Yes sir." The voice said.

"Well, the squad that dispatch sent my way turned out to be some guy named Poolside Tommy. He said he had killed my companion Charlie Foster. He pulled out a gun and tried to kill me too. But in the scuffle, I shot him instead."

"Is he dead?" The voice asked.

"I don't know," I responded. "But I left him laying in the road and came back to his house looking for help from the police that were sent here. When I got here, I found four of them unconscious, secured with their handcuffs to a tree. I also found my cousin Joe floating in a pool in the backyard. It seems the victim of an alligator attack."

I stopped talking and waited for a reply. There wasn't one at first. I then said into the radio, "Hello? You still there?"

The voice came back and replied, "Yes sir. Sorry, I was dispatching other units to your location. They are on their way now. Please wait for them and do not touch anything."

"Yes, of course." I said. "But you better send at least several EMT units too. Charlie, Duffy and Poolside Tommy will need attention. Not sure about your cops that are handcuffed and unconscious."

"Yes sir. They are on their way too, along with the coroner," the voice replied.

It wasn't more than 90 seconds later when I heard sirens heading in my direction…

Chapter Eighty-Five. Charlie

"What are you two doing here?"

I turned around to see George standing in the driveway with a gun. I grabbed Bob's arm looking for some reassurance and security. I could feel his forearm tighten as he clenched his fist.

"I would ask you the same thing, George." Said Bob.

"You're supposed to be dead. Both of you." George said. He looked angry and disappointed.

We could hear the sirens getting closer. "You're not that lucky," I said. "You should see what happened to Poolside Tommy."

Bob took a step closer to George.

"I wouldn't do that if I were you," said George as he cocked his gun.

Bob tried to reason with him. "Why are you doing this? You have everything. You don't need this."

"Don't I? You don't know everything. Your cousin thought he did. He got careless. Now look at him." He pointed his gun toward the back of the house where Joe was lying in the alligator pit. "And you, you had to get involved, Cousin Bob. If you knew what was good for you, you would have stayed in Ohio to finish that dumb deal."

"I still don't understand," said Bob.

"I wouldn't expect you to," said George. He put his finger on the trigger of the gun. "What I do expect is for you to put your hands up. It's time to head out back for a little family reunion."

I wasn't sure if any of this was real, or if I was dreaming, or maybe already dead. Although, if I were already dead this would be a weird afterlife. I looked up at Bob, waiting for his instruction. He looked down at me and stroked my arm. "Just go," he said. "We'll figure this out."

We turned around and walked toward the backyard. Something rustled in the bushes as we passed by. Probably a baby alligator. Why not? The gate of the fence was rusty. I felt like I might need a tetanus shot for looking at it. The pool was stained red. The air smelled weird. How did I end up back here?

At that point I realized I didn't hear the sirens. Did they go to the right place?

"Now for you two," George said. "I really didn't want it to come to this but you have left me with no choice."

He had us stand side-by-side. I could hear the news story now. "Two found dead, shot execution style next to an alligator pit." Why couldn't it at least be monkeys? I like monkeys. Or Flamingos. Monkeys and flamingos. There really is something wrong with me.
George pointed the gun, "Say bye-bye."

I closed my eyes and grabbed Bob's hand. "I love you." The gun went off. I felt Bob flinch as did I. I looked over at him. We were both standing.

George was still standing. What happened? Then George collapsed on the ground.

"Gotcha, feller," Danny appeared from behind. "That there is what I call a great shot."

Danny had a dumb grin on his face. "How do you keep doing that?" I said.

Danny shrugged his shoulders, "I guess I am smarter than I look."

Bob and I both laughed. We were still in shock at the scene around us, that we almost died…several times. And we were still unsure about what was happening. We heard some commotion coming from the front of the house. A man appeared around the side with his gun drawn, "put your hands up where I can see them."

It was the police. Thank God. Danny dropped his gun and we all put our hands above our heads. Once they figured out the scene was safe, they brought the paramedics and coroner in. The detective was taking everyone's report while the paramedics tended to our injuries.

"This is a mess," said the detective.

"Not really," said Danny. "I can tell you what happened real easy."

The detective looked at Danny incredulously.

"I would listen to him. He is smarter than he looks," I said.

"And sounds," added Bob.

"Alright, shoot." Said the detective.

"I'm out of bullets. I can't," said Danny.

The detective looked over at Bob and me impatiently. "Danny, just tell him what you know." I said.

"Oh, sure. That George feller owes some money to the mob. He got Joe in on that there deal to keep the county out of the way. Joe hated his job and saw it as a way to git out. Now that news feller Dusty picked up on it when the boss news guy over there at that TV station wouldn't let him do the story. Turns out his boss was gittin' a cut of the money if he done kept it out of the news."

Our jaws all hit the floor. "And how do you know this?" Asked the detective.

"That Dusty feller put a bug on me. Not like a real bug because that would have been gross, but like a listenin' and recordin' bug. People think I'm dumb so they tell me things."

"So you have proof of this?" Said the detective.

"Sure do. I've been wearin this here bug." Danny pulled up his shirt to show the wire.

"Where does Poolside Tommy fit into this?" Asked the detective.

"He be the mob hit man that George called in."

"This is crazy," said the detective. "I'm going to be here all night."

The paramedics weaved us in and out of the reporters camped out in the front yard. As the squad pulled out, Bob looked down and grabbed my hand, "I love you, too."

Chapter Eighty-Six. Bob

"Holy Crap!" I said as I looked at my watch. "It's almost 2 am! I'm supposed to be at work by 8. I have a 10 1/2 hour drive that I need to accomplish in just six hours. And all with no sleep either!"

"Can't you just call off again Bob?" Charlie asked, almost pleadingly.

"I wish I could," I replied. "But I don't have any more sick time that I can take. I used all my sick days taking my cat Boris to the vet and grooming appointments. If I don't get back, I may not have a job. And you know what that means don't you?"

"No Bob, I don't." Charlie said.

"Well, my dear. It means no job, no commission check. Part of the company's rules are that you have to be employed to receive commissions."

Looking for the detective, I asked, "Ok if I get out of here now? You got out of me everything I know."

The detective, not looking like he cared at all that I had places and commitments to get to, didn't even look up from his notes when he said, "Sure. Just make sure you're handy if I have anything more for you."

"You betcha." And as I looked at Charlie I continued, "I will be around for a good long time detective. A good long time."

Charlie softly said, "I hope so….."

_____

___

But for now, I gotta run! "Danny! Take care of Charlie for me while I'm gone. Shouldn't be for more than a couple of weeks or so!"

"You got 'er chief," Danny replied with new found confidence. "She be safe with me."

I got into my Jeep and went tearing out of East Lake toward the direction of Cleveland. Knowing I wasn't going to make it in time, I called my boss's voicemail at work and left a message.

"Uh, hi, boss. This is Bob. I know I told you I'd be in today. Well, I will be. I'm just going to be running a bit late. Should be in before lunch. Sorry! See you then!"

I hung up the cell phone and focused on getting back to Ohio as quickly as I could. I knew I would have no time for sleep. Just have to do that when I got to my desk, I thought. The sheer absurdity of it made me giggle a bit. The only stops I would be able to make is for gas. Not even time for the bathroom. And I still didn't know how I was going to explain the arm bandaged by the EMT at Poolside Tommy's before leaving.

The sun was starting to peak over the horizon to my east as I drove north on Interstate 95 at the Fredericksburg exit. Only about six and half hours to go. Going to be pushing it to be there by noon. Closer to 1 pm will be more likely. I told my boss I'd be in by lunch. Just gonna be a late lunch, I told myself.

After driving all the previous day and all through the night and the next morning I was exhausted when I pulled the Jeep into my parking space at the back of the building. The clock on my dashboard told me it was 12:47. As I got to the back door, I realized that I had left my key fob to the building at home, so I had to walk around to the front, where I ran into a gaggle of those "Oh, we're so happy to be here people milling around in the lobby." As I passed them, under my breath I muttered "damn sheep." I raced to my desk under those blasted florescent lights to find my boss sitting in my chair. Uh oh. This ain't good…..

"Hello sausage guy. Feeling better I trust." He said.

"Um. Yeah. Fever seemed to have broken. Didn't get much sleep last night. But I'm here. Just as I promised."

"I see that." He replied, as he eyed my bandaged arm. "And since when do we come to work in shorts, t-shirt, and flip-flops?" He asked.

"Well, sir." SIR! That word just doesn't flow freely with me, and deep down I knew that he knew that it didn't. "Well sir," I continued. "As I said, I didn't sleep all that well last night and I didn't have any clean clothes at home," I lied.

"Sausage guy, you can cut the charade," he said. "You weren't sick and the only reason you didn't get any sleep is because you drove the entire night back from the Outer Banks."

How can he know that, I wondered. Still I better not admit anything too readily.

"Let me ask you…." The bossman said. "Watch the news this morning?"

"Um, no. Should I have?" I asked.

"Only if you wanted to see yourself, you should've," he replied.

For a few long seconds I didn't say anything, but then managed to squeak out, "Oh?"

"Yeah. Big news story plastered everywhere this morning. Must have been a slow news day since the top story was about a couple of murders in East Lake, North Carolina. Seems a guy even got eaten by an alligator. What do you know about that sausage guy?"

"Um, nothing. Why?"

"Well, I reckon. That's how you say it in the Carolina's, reckon, right? Well, no matter. I reckon the guy eaten by the alligator was your kin. Guy named Joe. Worked for the county."

"Oh really?" I said. "What does that have to do with me?"

"Well, I wondered that too, sausage guy. At first I thought it was just a coincidence. But my boss told me to look at the footage of the scene a little bit more closely. And since I always listen to my boss, without having to spit out the word sir, I did. Know what I saw sausage guy?"

Knowing that I was apparently busted, I still decided to play dumb. So I replied, "Reckon you're gonna tell me."

"Yes sir. I am. Seems that while the local TV station was interviewing the Dare County detective about the crime, there you were in the background with some girl and some slack jaw hillbilly."

"Now wait a minute!" I yelled. "Danny ain't no slack jaw hillbilly. Well at first I thought he was, but he just happened to be the guy who saved quite a few lives last night. So I'll ask you to not refer to him that way."

"Ok Sausage guy. Ok. But you do admit to being there then?"

Knowing I didn't have any other way to answer at this point, I said, "yes."

The bossman didn't say anything at first. He just sat in my desk chair rocking it back and forth. Finally after a couple of minutes he said, "Well sir. You have left me no choice. While you were "sick" (he air quoted the word sick), the nursing home called several times with some questions. We didn't have the answers to give them because you didn't take the time to write the sale up properly. You have not made your job your priority since your vacation. I have to let you go. I have no other choice in the matter....."

"You're firing me?" I exclaimed.

"No Bob (he never calls me Bob), you fired yourself. This was a huge account and you did not service it properly."

"This is just this effing company's way of not having to pay a commission on this sale. You money grubbing bitches. You know that I don't deserve to be fired. You just have no backbone to stand up for yourself, let alone me, and do what's right! This damn company is all about the money, and if they can save one single penny, they have no problems throwing me overboard. I expect that will happen to you one day too!"

"No sir. It will not happen to me." The boss said. "Know why?" Answering his own question, he went on. "I'll tell you why, because I come in here and make these 9 to 10 hours a commitment in my life. That is something you have never done. You just go by the rules you want to go by. You never partook in company outings. You never participated in company town halls. You were just Bob Evans. The hell with everyone else!"

"You know what?" I asked. "Baa!"

"Baa?"

"Yeah. Baa. You damn sheep. Live your life like you're going to slaughter. I'm outta here." I turned and started for the door.

Calling after me the ex-boss said, "What about your building key fob? I need that back!"

Over my shoulder I yelled back, "Yeah, this company can't afford losing a fob. Take it out of my last check prick."

I pushed open the back door on my way out, I thought I may have broken it as I did. Probably take that out of my check too, I thought. I stormed to my Jeep, turned on the ignition and said to myself, "Oh hell. Adios Ohio. Hello North Carolina!"

Chapter Eighty-Seven. ABC 11

Good evening folks and welcome to a special edition of ABC news at 6. My name is Frank Hologram — let's get this thing started.

For most of the people in our viewing area you know we've been following the story of local restaurant owner, Charlie Foster, and the selling of the Nags Head pier that ended in a slam bang finish nearly eight weeks ago. Tonight we welcome back one of our most esteemed colleagues. Reporting live for the first time in two months, we go to Duffy Dixon live at the Nags Head pier. Duffy.

Thank you, Frank. Let me tell you folks it feels great to be back holding this microphone and I could not have asked for a better first assignment than giving an update on the Nags Head pier. As most of you know, I was involved in an accident that nearly ended my life. I was grateful to be alive after the accident but I was also in a very dark place. Then Charlie Foster walked in my hospital room. And she continued to do so everyday until I was out of the hospital. Then she came to my house along with Bob Evans, not the sausage guy. They cooked and cleaned and did my yard work. No one asked them to do it. It's that kind of generosity that Nags Head needs. We can't afford to lose people like that so I am here to pay it forward. So if you don't mind following me to Chuck's, my assistant is trying to get Charlie out here for an interview. This way, please.

And there she is, Charlie Foster.

"Hey Duffy. It's nice to see you with your microphone again."

Thank you, Charlie, It's nice to be back. We are giving an update on the Nags Head pier situation. Can you tell us what you know?

"Sure, but there isn't much to tell. I lost the ukulele contest to Sandy Butts, whom is very talented, by the way. She will be headed to Savannah as part of the tour. I suggest you all check it out, I know I will. But nothing has happened with the pier since the scandal broke so we are still operating until we hear otherwise."

I am here to tell you otherwise, Charlie. We here at ABC 11 are bringing you a special report with breaking news.

"Duffy, if I'm going to get angry, I don't want the cameras on me. Two viral videos are enough."

The pier has been sold…to me as of 12pm today.

"Shut up. You're not serious."

I am. After the station manager was fired, I was promoted. I have wanted to own this pier since I was a little boy. It's why I tried and failed to be part of the deal, but now we know why George wouldn't let that happen. So with my bonus, raise, and savings I bought the pier and I am willing to sell you your restaurant location for a fair price.

"I don't have any money, Duffy."

For 1 dollar, Charlie. It's yours fair and square.

"Are you serious?"

Completely. Thank you for being a role model and such a pillar in our community. I wish you nothing but the best. Oh, and I am having the mechanical shark put back in your restaurant.

"I don't know what to—"

Don't. To commemorate this moment, I got a coffee mug for you: WHAT THE FRAK? CHUCK GOT HER RESTAURANT BACK!

"I think I'm gonna cry…"